A WOMAN WILD

A WOMAN WILD

A Novel

Barbara Williams Lewis

ALAMO BAY PRESS

SEADRIFT•AUSTIN

Copyright © 2025 by Barbara Williams Lewis

All rights reserved. No part of this book may be reproduced in any form without permission in writing from the publisher, except by a reviewer who may quote brief passages in a review.

Cover: Patricia Erikson. *Used with permission of the artist.*
Author Photograph: Barbara Williams Lewis
Book Design: ABP

Alamo Bay Press
Pamela Booton, Director
Lowell Mick White, Editor
Diane Wilson, Activist

For orders and information:
Alamo Bay Press
825 W 11th Ste 114
Austin, Texas 78701
pam@alamobaypress.com
www.alamobaypress.com

Library of Congress Control Number: 2025945134
Paperback ISBN: 978-1-943306-33-6

For

Paralynn, Tatia, Jeremy, and Shanada.
You are the best I have ever done.

She is free in her wildness, she is a wanderess,
a drop of free water. She knows nothing of
borders and cares nothing for rules or customs.
"Time" for her isn't something to fight against.
Her life flows clean, with passion, like fresh
water.

   —Roman Payne, The Wanderess

A WOMAN WILD

Foreword	xiii
Prologue: Tuesday August 17, 1915	1
Part One: Lula	5
Part Two: Lula B.	65
Part Three: Easter	103
Part Four: Beulah	135
Part Five: Barbara	193
Afterword	213
Acknowledgments	217
About Barbara Lewis Williams	219

A WOMAN WILD

Foreword

THE WRITING OF *SHERROD VILLAGE* WAS A PASSIONATE enterprise. I labored over it, nursed it and dismissed the idea time and time again, only to come back to it after more than thirty years of thinking about it. The thought haunted me all that time, yet I knew that eventually I would be brave enough to tell someone that story. Indeed, there were parts that I missed and events that I left out intentionally, but when I finished the book, I knew I wanted to write more and to re-visit the people in my life who have most influenced me.

My greatest regret is that I did not pay more attention to my father when he tried to guide me and prepare me for life. Like many young folks I saw little value in discussing past hurts, past wrongs, past history. I especially resented him for trying to explain his treatment of my mother. It was always in the heat of a moment when he had abused her in public—a wedding or funeral—that he wanted to tell me his side of a story. I should have taken pen to paper right then, but I wanted no part of it. I wanted the argument to end, and the truth is, I wanted to escape. That was the only way I could make it all better for me. Just get away and let them handle their problems. I thought then as I think now, the worst thing a married couple can do is fight in front of their children. My sister once said, "We are who we are because they are who they are." That made perfect sense, and I eventually loosened up a bit. By the time I got around to the desire to listen to them, however, they were both gone.

They are still very much a part of me though, and I do not know who to credit or who to blame for the person I am. I stepped out of the shower one day long ago and stood gazing at my image in the mirror, reflecting on how I came to be who I am. It was a moment of vulnerability. I began to interrogate my position in this great universe. *Who am I? Why am I here? Why can't I be more like "normal" people? Why am I such a rebel?* These are the kinds of questions that come with the recognition that the only way one's life can change is if he or she makes that move. It is the hardest thing anyone will ever have to do. On that day I thought to myself, *I am who I am,* and I had worked hard to recognize and accept my own identity. I had anguished over it. Prayed, even. My father called me wild. My mother called me lazy. My sister said I was a natural born rebel, but even she knew that any changes I made to myself to satisfy others would present a counterfeit Barbara.

This caused me to look back into my history and examine the lives of my ancestors. I was brought up close to my mother's family. I wanted to find my father's mother again and to know more about her life and her parents and theirs. I wanted to resurrect them, breathe life into them and yes, thank them for being so much a part of me. Most pressing was the concept of writing them and myself *free.*

So, I present this writing to you in the spirit of truth, honesty, and integrity. In my search I have learned that my sister was right. I was born into rebellion. I was bred for it.

Prologue: Tuesday August 17, 1915

IN THE EARLY MORNING HOURS OF THIS DAY, JOHN DAVIES started his drive home. He had just left Bee's house and, satisfied to the bone, he was enjoying a leisurely ride. He noticed the purples and greys of a new day coming as the sun had just begun to brighten the horizon; the delicious smell of air was pure as a newborn babe. Squirrels scurried about in search of breakfast and the clop of Ginny's feet was the background to the happy tune John whistled.

He was in no hurry. His wife, Ellen, would be upset surely because he had been gone all night. But the warmth in his heart was more than enough ammunition to ward off her attack. Bee Cooper was his real woman. She was the one the sun rose to see. Their family together was growing and John was very proud. He was equally proud of the way Bee made him feel. There was never a schedule. There was never hesitation. Her willingness and spontaneity always excited him.

Last night was no different. He had planned to go home, but he was caught in a kind of trance when he was in Bee's arms. The touch of her skin, the smell of her hair, the freshness of her bed always had the feeling of *home.*

He noticed the light on at the General Store on

Highway 58. It was not quite six in the morning, and since it was much too early for hunting season, and the store did not open until seven, it caused him to slow his horse. He saw some of his friends waiting there, and he decided to stop and inquire about the matter. He stepped off the seat of his buckboard and looped the reins to his horse around the bar.

"Morning," he said to the waiting men. "What y'all doing out here so early? What's wrong?"

One of the men spat tobacco juice on John's shoes. "You what's wrong, John. We out here waiting for you."

"For me? Why?"

"'Cause we need to talk to you. Try to talk some sense into you one last time."

"Humph. Talk sense to me? About what?"

"We need to talk to you about you and that colored gal. You done lost your goddamn mind."

"You mean Lula B.?"

"That's right."

"How many times do I have to say this? That is *my* business. Y'all ain't got nothing to do with it."

"Now, see, that there is where you wrong, John. Your wife talks to our wives. That makes things hard on us. We can't go nowhere. Can't do nothing. They all scared we gon' follow in your footsteps. So that makes it our business. We in this. All of us."

By now three other men had arrived and the crowd swelled to a dozen or so. They were armed with sticks, shovels and rocks. One had a rope and another had a shotgun.

"Like I said, it ain't your business. And show some respect. She's not a gal; she is my woman. Now you boys just go on home and stop worrying about what I'm doing."

The men looked at each other. John looked to the sky. By now the sun was in full view.. It would be a good day. He eyed the men steadily for a moment and took a deep breath. "You boys go on home now," he repeated.

John turned his back and headed towards his horse. The first blow to his head knocked him down. As he reached for his knife, he felt a boot kick in his ribs. The pain went to his stomach and exploded around his back. John Davies was no match for the angry mob that attacked him. He was bleeding and on the ground. He covered his head with his hands to try to fend off the blows.

His thoughts were on Bee—laughing, singing, her hair blowing in the wind. He remembered how much he loved her and their children. The joy he felt when he was with her. The games she used to play. The wonder in her eyes when he presented her with some trinket. The sweetness of her lips. He thought of the day they met. She was so young. So beautiful. So happy to belong to him. "Bee...Bee..." he whispered.

The men continued to hit him again and again. He tasted the blood as it poured from his mouth. It only lasted a few short minutes, but when the beating was over, John was dead. His friends loaded him onto his buckboard, hit Ginny on the ass and sent John Davies home to his wife.

Part One

Lula

One

In the winter of 1841, twelve-year-old Annie lay laboring on a bed made of chicken feathers and corn husks just outside what is now Pine Tops, North Carolina. She had lost her mucus plug two days before, but there was still no water and no baby. Her screams could be heard through the woods all the way to the big house. Susan, the cook for the Cooper Plantation, busied herself dabbing snow on the forehead of the feverish child. The wind howled and banked the snow against the little cabin. The windows clattered as if they were talking to each other, as if they knew of the horror that was happening in that room.

Mazzie, the mid-wife, checked to see if Annie was close to delivery. She, too, was young, only a year or so older than Annie. When she felt a foot instead of a head, she gasped and nearly fainted.

"I can't do this!" she said. "I never seen anything like it in my whole life. I don't know what to do."

"You can and you will," said Susan. "What's the matter?"

"The baby upside down."

"Well turn it around. And hurry up!"

"All right. All right." She took a deep breath and moved her hand clumsily into the screaming child. "Don't push, Annie."

There was a knock on the door and Susan answered. Sam came in with a load of wood and went straight to the stove. "Look like I come right on time," he said. "This fire near 'bout gone out."

Susan and Mazzie had not noticed. All they could think about was poor Annie. She was having such a time with this, her first born. It really was not fair. She was too young, too tender for her little body to suffer such violation. Mr. Fleming had traded her for a bottle of whiskey. Aside from the pain of being "broke in" by a drunken white man, she had to endure the indignation of bearing his seed.

Susan wiped her hands on a towel and poured Sam some coffee. "What you doing down here in this weather?"

"Miss Martha want to know if Annie foal yet."

"Naw, not yet. Sun's 'bout to go down, too. Be dark in a minute. Looks like we gon' have another long night."

"Miss Martha said do you want me to go over to Toisnot and get old Doc Simmons?"

"Doc Simmons? The horse doctor?"

"Yes'm."

"Naw."

"You sure now? Miss Martha said that screaming is keeping her awake at night."

"I'm sure. Besides, the snow is so deep the horses can't get through."

"Yes'm. I'll tell her that." He tipped his hat and left.

Annie's screams died down to small whimpers. She was too weak, Susan thought, to protest the vicious attack on her body. Mazzie worked diligently to turn the baby, but when a leg popped out, she quickly abandoned her project.

So did Annie. She simply rolled her eyes to the back of her head and expelled a breath she had not taken. Susan plunged her arm elbow-deep into Annie and snatched the child from her lifeless cave. The baby gurgled and snorted as she struggled for her first breath.

She weighed more than twelve pounds and she was

over twenty-two inches long. Susan named her Lula. It would turn out to be a very fitting name

Susan had no children of her own. She never wanted any. On the few occasions that she got caught she quickly used a potion of castor oil and vinegar to fix the problem. Now, alone with this child, she felt the desire to nurture her. The kind of closeness anyone can feel for an abandoned puppy. She wrapped the baby in a blanket and fixed her a sugar tit to suck, holding her close to her heart for the rest of the night.

By morning the snow had stopped. Susan gave the baby another sugar tit and heated some water to wash Annie. She bathed the dead girl all over and rubbed her with olive oil. Then she looked around the cabin for something with which she could perfume the body. At long last she settled on a little dried lavender that she, herself, had used in her bath. She wrapped Annie's body in a clean sheet and left her on the bed.

The sun was blinding bright and the sound of the snow melting was almost musical. Susan folded a blanket around the baby, tucked her under her own wrap and took the child with her to the big house. Trudging through the snow, she hummed a tune as Lula started to whimper: *Quand tu seras plus age, tu n'auras plus de larmes.* It meant, "When you are older, you will have no more tears."

Mazzie stood at the stove shamed-faced. "It's a girl," Susan said. "A great ol' big one."

"Where's Annie?"

"She's gone."

"What you gon' do with that young'un?"

"Well, I was thinking...Suki just had a baby. So did Maybelle. Maybe they can take turns feeding her."

Martha came into the kitchen just in time to hear Susan say that Annie was gone. "What do you mean she's gone?"

"She died, Miss Martha. There wasn't anything I could do. I am so sorry."

Martha broke down and cried. In a moment she was as composed as ever. She looked at the baby. "Is it a boy or girl?"

"It's a girl, Ma'am."

"Oh my. What shall we do with her?"

"Well, I was hoping we could keep her right here. I'll take care of her."

Martha unwrapped the blanket so she could get a better look. "Good Lord! She's a big one. No wonder Annie—." She wiped her nose and lifted the child. "Sure, she can stay here. Annie's old cradle is upstairs. There are some diapers up there, too. You go get them while I sit here and hold this baby."

"Yes, Ma'am. You know Miss Martha ...I was thinking that maybe we could cook a lamb for next Sunday dinner. To celebrate, you know."

"Yes. Yes, that will be fine. Now run along. Mazzie, go tell Suki to come here right away. This big girl needs to eat something. And tell Sam to dig a hole for poor little Annie."

Sam was Martha Fleming's special slave. He was sixteen, strong as any animal, and he was light-skinned with curly hair. Mrs. Fleming kept him close to her, especially when Mr. Fleming was away on business. She secretly taught him how to read and write so that he could go into Toisnot and do her shopping. She also let him sleep on a pallet on the kitchen floor during the winter months. It was warm there, and the last thing she wanted was for him to catch cold. Everybody in the quarters knew about this special relationship, yet nobody told Mr. Fleming or Mr. Donovan, the Irish overseer. It was a well-kept secret and the keeping of it served to protect everyone.

Before Sam there was Ed, and before him there was Benny. In each case somebody saw and somebody told. Benny mysteriously disappeared, never to be seen or heard from again. But they did find out what happened to Ed and it was so horrible that nobody ever told Mr. Fleming anything again. Even when they were dripping wet and he asked if it was raining, they would say, "I don't know, Suh."

Mr. Fleming moved to one of the downstairs bedrooms when he found out about Benny. After Ed, he refused to even sit at the dining table with Mrs. Fleming, so he took his meals in his room. Word spread through the quarters that the only reason he did not make Mrs. Fleming disappear was that she was the one with the money. The house was hers, the land was hers, but Mr. Fleming was the one with sense enough to manage it all. So he tolerated her indiscretions with the knowledge that anyone important would never know the truth. Slaves were not important.

Charles Cooper had fought in the Revolutionary War. Because Martha was his only child, he doted on her. He taught her how to read and write, insisting that a girl child needed to know the ways of the world in order to protect herself. He introduced her to the classics: Shakespeare, Dante, Sophocles, and in a time when most women had no voice, he encouraged her to speak her mind. His own wife, Martha's mother, had completely subscribed to the notion that women should be seen and not heard. On the one hand, this was an attribute that he admired when they were in public, but it caused him to never know what she was thinking, and this caused him much distress over time.

Charles Cooper's greatest desire was to accumulate property that he could bequeath to his daughter. He wanted to be sure that she would never be dependent upon a man to support her. He was a professional soldier, was willing to fight for any just cause, and just before he went off to war again, he told Martha: "One day you will take a husband. Don't think for a minute that you have to be at his mercy. If something happens and the marriage does not last, *he* will be the one to go; this is *your* home."

He loved to collect unusual things that he found in nature—fossils, petrified tree limbs, and especially rocks. On one of his various trips throughout the state he found a chert quarry and he bought a wagon load of it and spread it across his front yard. The mixture of the colors in the rock—grey, red, white and brown—excited him and he was impressed that no one else recognized its beauty. He also built most of his furniture. In fact, he built the house in which Martha was born. It was three stories tall with large columns on the front. There was a veranda that circled the second floor and each room on that floor opened to it. The front porch had a swing on one end, and two rocking chairs and a table on the other. The house was white with black shutters, and he painted the front door red. The entire top floor was at first a nursery—pink, yellow and white. As Martha grew into a young girl, her father painted the rooms red, Martha's favorite color. He built a desk and chair and placed them by the window. On the south side he built a bookshelf that covered the entire wall, and he kept it stocked with fine books. Her bed faced the east, and it was surrounded by white curtains and piled high with red pillows. This was her haven, her spot, and aside from an occasional cleaning by Clara, only Susan was allowed to visit there. When Charles was killed in the war of 1812, Martha inherited the house, 120 slaves and more than 2,500 acres of land. She was only ten years old.

Mrs. Cooper died in 1814. No one knew her ailment, but she took sick on Tuesday and died on Thursday. As Clara and others busied themselves making arrangements for the funeral, Martha looked on with interest. Her life was not changed by this regrettable fact.

When she was seventeen Martha met and married Flannigan Fleming. He was an itinerant gambler with a head full of ambition and good business sense to go with it. He was tall and handsome with red hair and green eyes, and while Martha did not feel the thunder of heaven rolling in her chest when she met him, she was fascinated by the way he took control of any given situation. They met on a hot, sunny afternoon when Martha was taking her daily ride. She drove into the sun and, at first, she could only see the silhouette of the approaching rider. In her attempt to make room for the stranger on the narrow road, she steered her carriage to the right, so far that the horses, seeing the danger of the ditch, lurched to the left and all but threw her off the buggy. The incident caused a broken wheel on the carriage, and Flannigan dismounted to examine it.

He tipped his hat. "Afternoon, Ma'am."

"It's not Ma'am. It's Miss. Miss Martha Cooper."

He nodded and raised his brows, a little surprised by her arrogance. "Looks like you have a little problem. Mind if I take a look?"

"Suit yourself."

It was not a difficult task to see that the wheel could not be fixed. Three spokes were broken, and the wheel was dislodged from the axle. Still, he took his time pretending to fix it. He smiled to himself as he noticed the restlessness in her. She shifted on her seat, fanned herself and tried unsuccessfully to appear disinterested in what he was doing. At long last he said, "Well, this here is going to take some fixing that I am not equipped to do. Can I give you a lift somewhere?"

Martha deliberated her options: take a ride from this stranger or walk a mile in this heat. She waved her fan rapidly past her face. "If it's no trouble," she said.

"Oh no trouble at all, *Miss* Cooper."

He lifted her off the buggy, placed her side saddle onto his horse and delivered her directly home.

Once there Martha invited him to stay for dinner as a means of repayment for his kindness. She insisted that he take a downstairs bedroom so he could refresh himself before leaving in the morning. But when morning came, she gave him breakfast and by dinner she had offered him a job.

As Martha had hoped, Flannigan was a natural at running a plantation and within three months they were married. But Martha learned on her wedding night that his mind only had room for business. He was not tender or affectionate; he was deliberate, brutal, and quick. She felt compelled to speak on it.

"Is that it?"

"What?"

"Is that all there is to it?"

"What are you talking about, woman?"

"Well, I have had conversations with my married friends and they are all excited about the times they spend with their husbands. I mean—in the night."

"And?"

"And I don't understand what all the excitement is about. What you just did hurt me all over."

"Well, it's like that the first time. It'll get better."

"Promise?"

"Promise."

She wanted to try again, but he had work to do in the morning and he needed to rest. So she waited.

Over the next few weeks and months, Mr. and Mrs. Fleming did try over and over again. And though the pain eventually subsided, the results were the same. Before long she started to deny him his husbandly rights. They argued over that, her headaches, her stomach aches, her menses. After a while, he just stopped asking.

Then one day when Mr. Fleming was away, Martha stood at the window and watched Benny as he loaded the barn with hay. He was shirtless and sweaty, and as the sun shone on his body, she thought of a Greek god. She found herself fondling her nipples, and when she could no longer stand the breathlessness, she poured a glass of lemonade and took it to Benny. She invited him into the shade of the barn to drink it. He thanked her kindly, and when he turned to go back to work, she threw her arms around his neck. She could feel him stiffen, partly because of fear and partly because of desire.

"Miss Martha...Ma'am...please...don't...."

She opened his trousers and touched him. He felt his own betrayal in her hand. He lifted her onto a bale of hay, and soon Martha discovered the secret all of her girlfriends knew.

When Susan returned with the cradle and diapers, Suki was there feeding the child and Martha was gone.

"Did she say anything?" she asked Mazzie.

"About what?"

"About Sunday."

"No. Why?"

"I didn't quite tell her the whole truth. We will have a naming ceremony for this child."

"A naming *ceremony?*"

"Yes. It is called *Aqiqah.*"

"What you gon' name her?"

"Lula."

'Lula? Where'd you get that plinkety name?"

"It's not plinkety. It's Irish. It means *abundance, lady princess*. It also means *fearless warrior.*"

There was an awkward moment of silence as Mazzie witnessed a gleam in Susan's eye she had never seen.

"How you know that?"

"I just know things."

"But you don't even like young'uns."

"Never said I don't like 'em. I just never wanted any."

"Why not?"

"That ought to be plain enough to you. Didn't Mr. Fleming take your boy, Coot, and send him to Raleigh last year?"

"What's that got to do with this?"

"That's what they do. I didn't want that to happen to a child of mine. I know what it feels like to be separated from your mama. It happened to me."

Recognizing an unusual mellow moment for Susan, Mazzie pressed for more.

"When? I thought you were born here. I thought Clara was your mama."

"I *was* born here, but Abby was *sama yaay*. I did not see her as often as I wanted. She worked long, hard days in the fields. Clara was the cook then. She's the one who raised me. She taught me the ways of white folks.

But I learned about life from my own mama. I learned how to raise children and I learned how to never have any." Susan waved her hand as if to dismiss any further questions from Mazzie. "Hand me one of them diapers. This baby done made a mess already."

Susan poured water from a pitcher into a basin and washed Lula with her hands. Then she folded the diaper into a triangle and covered the child's bottom, tucking in the ends to secure it. As she laid the baby down for a nap she whispered to her, *La, la, mon enfant. Je suis sure que tout va bien s'epasser."*

On Sunday morning, Susan arose early and started to prepare the food. She made a sauce for the lamb with honey and lemon. She made a big chocolate cake, and she said a prayer for Annie. It had been a week since she died, and Susan's biggest task was to shave Lula's head on that day. It was a tradition her mother had taught her as she passed on the rudiments of Islam. Abby was one of the few on the plantation who were never Christianized. Mr. Cooper had given her sanction to practice whatever religion she chose as long as she believed in *something*. So she kept her traditions and taught them to Susan every chance she got.

Shaving Lula's head had to be done when she was one week old. Exactly. And Susan had expected resistance from the child. Instead, Lula slept through the entire ritual. When the lamb was done and everyone gathered, Susan proudly presented Lula Cooper to the community. Suki made potato salad. Maybelle brought baked sweet potatoes and mustard greens. The women all dressed in colorful clothing and scarves. They made music with homemade flutes, dried gourds and pots and pans. They danced and ate and sang all afternoon. How they all laughed! Even Miss Martha seemed to be having a good time.

Two

With the help of Susan, Suki and Maybelle, Lula grew into a fine child. From the beginning she was different from most babies. She crawled at five months old and she walked at seven. She did not reach and grab for food unless it was presented to her on purpose. She never peed the bed, and at fifteen months she toilet trained herself. It was almost like she had been here before, Susan thought. Like she knew how to go through life on her own without instructions from anyone. There was a wildness in her that would not be tamed. She took her food with her left hand, for example, and she had a tendency to ignore people she did not like. She didn't like the *kitchie kitchie koo* game, and she never laughed. Once in a while it looked like she was going to crack a smile, but her bottom lip quickly turned upside down. Throughout her childhood Lula had no interest in doing the traditional *girly* things; she did not like to cook or sew. And while Sam had whittled a doll for her and Mazzie made it a dress, Lula refused to play with it.

Lula was not pretty like most babies; her face looked like a grown woman's face from the start. She had bronze-colored skin with dark brown freckles, and she had flaming red hair. The good thing about her, though, was that she was strong and hard-working. Tall for her age. Sturdy. In the evenings when the slaves all gathered around the campfire and sang, all the other children felt comfort in placing their heads in their mothers' laps and drifting off to sleep. Not Lula. She would find a tree to climb or a stick to draw in the dirt. Horses were her favorite. She would draw horses with long, bushy tails, their heads high in majestic fashion.

Susan gave up on the notion of coddling Lula. She saw the child's independence as a good thing. "Any child ain't got no mama got to be in a whole lot of pain," she said. So they let her be. Lula was free to do whatever she pleased.

At four she was cropping tobacco in the summer and picking cotton in the fall. She preferred working in the fields. By six she could beat the boys at everything— fighting, fishing, killing rabbits and squirrels. As far as anyone could tell, Lula took only one lesson—just one— from a boy named Joe Lee. He taught her how to make a bow. She made her own arrows after that and, smashing a piece of chert against a rock, she was able to make the arrowheads and tie them on with hemp. She also made a fishing pole and used a safety pin as a hook. The safety pin was a new invention and Miss Martha was constantly shopping for the most modern household gadgets. It worked perfectly to snag fish. A piece of chicken liver or a squirrel heart was excellent bait for the hungry bass that lived in the irrigation pond.

Lula hunted and fished every day. Susan took great pride in her fried rabbit and the Brunswick stew she made with the squirrels. The child took pride in eating the food that she herself had provided.

She couldn't sit still long enough for schooling. Instead, she preferred to take her lessons from living. Surviving. She determined to create a space that was hers alone, and the fact that she was a girl never interfered with the way she wanted to live her life. Lula would climb hills and stand at the top of them, reigning over the entire land. She talked to the trees, the birds and the rocks. She loved to dance, and she was good at it. Raising her arms and twirling, twirling, her eyes closed, her face to the sun, she danced in honor of its warmth. She celebrated every single morning, and she found joy in her accomplishments at the end of each day.

One day during this ritual she sensed that she was being watched.

It was Joe Lee.

"What you doing up here, Joe?"

"Oh, I just came to keep you company."

"This is my hill. I got all the company I want."

"You mean them birds?" He laughed a little.

"I mean all of it. It belongs to me."

"It belong to Miss Martha."

"Well, she own the real. The spirit of it belong to me!"

He could detect the anger rising in her and that was not his purpose. He loved her, had loved her since the day she let him instruct her on how to make a bow. He had to figure out a way to calm her.

"How old you be, Lula?"

"Fifteen. Best I can figure."

"'Bout time for you to be thinking 'bout finding yo'self a man, ain't it?"

"A man? For what?"

"Somebody to love you."

"Who gon' love me? I'm ugly."

"Ugly? Who told you that?"

"Nobody had to tell me. I look in the glass. I can see."

"Maybe you ain't looking for the right thing."

"What you mean?"

"I mean...a woman don't know how to look at herself, or any other woman for that matter. A woman needs to be looked at with a man's eye. One might have a pretty face, but the other one has nice ankles."

"You mean you don't see ugly when you look at me?"

He shook his head. "I don't see ugly nowhere."

Because she did not look like anyone else on the plantation, Lula accepted the thought that she was not pretty. This knowledge helped her live a life free of pretense and distraction. Now, Joe Lee's comments confused her. She sat down by an old oak tree and beckoned him to join her.

"What do you see?"

"I see a woman. A woman with strong arms and legs and wide saddle hips. Perfect for making babies."

"Uh uh. I don't want no chil'ren."

"Why not?"

"I just don't that's all."

Joe Lee got up to leave. "Well, if you change yo' mind—"

"Ain't gon' change my mind. I ain't gon' change nothing!"

So, Joe Lee left her on that hill. As he walked away shaking his head, he muttered to himself, "What kind of woman is this? Don't want no chil'ren?"

Lula never bothered with bloomers; she saw them as cumbersome. The women who wore them had to stop what they were doing and go find a private spot to relieve themselves. She, however, could simply lift her skirt, spread her legs and pee wherever she happened to be. She could continue her work and shake her lily dry in the process. When she rested, she sat wide-legged on the porch steps. Susan once said to her, "Put some drawers on!"

"She likes to be free," Lula responded.

"Well let *her* be free in your house," Susan said. "That bird needs a cage."

Since Lula had no mother, she had no sense of direction, and Susan's advice was often ignored— dismissed as a part of a generation of etiquette that used to be. She saw Susan bathing in the pond one day, and as she watched the old woman lift her breasts Lula shouted, "That's got to be the longest goddamn titty I ever saw!" They both laughed. "Wait 'til you get older, Susan said. "You got a perky set right now, but when you get my age they will be cushions for your knees when you work."

Still, the women admired Lula; the girls thought she was disgusting. The boys envied her; the men declared that something was wrong. "A whistling woman and a crowing hen always come to some bad end," they chanted. And Lula could whistle better than anyone on the Cooper Plantation.

Lula was never sick—not even a cold. In fact, it was Lula who laid hands on the puny and made them better. She'd make a paste of roots and herbs and hog tallow and place it on a congested chest. Then she'd lay a hot towel on the infected area and make sounds that no one understood—not really words, but a combination of grunts and syllables, a chant of gibberish, indeed, but it always worked. Within the hour her patient would cough up the offensive substance. The grateful mothers paid her with gifts of cobblers, peach preserves, cowries or chopped wood.

Yes, Lula was gifted. She could do it all. Most folks loved her, but even those who hated her loved her exceptional capabilities.

●

Lula, in turn, loved no one. Since her own mother didn't care enough to stick around, she had no idea what the word meant. She had seen the devastation that love could bring. When Maybelle's man was sold, Lula had watched the old woman wither away to nothing. Maybelle looked like her soul had been snatched right out of her. She lost her hair and she refused to eat anything. Eventually she became so weak that she could not even walk. She grieved herself to death.

So Lula forced love to keep its distance—far away from her. In that way she would never have to face the hurt and disappointment she had seen in others when love failed them.

But something *was* missing and she felt empty, unfulfilled, not quite complete. Maybe Joe Lee was right. Maybe she was due—overdue even—to discover what a man could offer her. But he would be a man of her choosing, not an overly obvious volunteer like Joe Lee. *She* would choose.

She chose Jim, a boy with whom she had worked the fields. There was not much about him in the way of looks, but she had noticed on more than one occasion that he frequently had a pup tent protruding from his pants. She found him in the fields suckling tobacco. When she approached him with a smile on her face, she stroked the hard muscle on his forearm. He smiled back.

He said, "You want to gi' me some don't you?"

She said, "Yes, I do."

He said, "When?"

She said, "Now."

He said, "Where?"

She said, "How 'bout right here?"

It was just that simple. They lay down in the tobacco field and Lula let him guide her into womanhood.

The next day Mrs. Fleming sent for her. At first, she thought it might have something to do with Jim, so she went in prepared to defend herself. She was a little skeptical of Mrs. Fleming. Something about her made Lula nervous. Perhaps it was the way the old woman covertly stared at her when she thought Lula was not looking. They never talked, but Lula felt a strange kind of closeness to her. Kindred spirits with a chemistry that charged each of them and offered a sense of freedom.

Mrs. Fleming was having a cup of tea in the parlor and she offered Lula a seat.

"No...Ma'am...I thank you."

"It's all right, Lula. I have invited you to have a seat in my home. It would be rude to refuse. Sit down."

Lula sat on the edge of her chair. Colored people were never invited to sit down in white folks' houses. She did not know what to expect. She felt defenseless as she sat. What if Miss Martha tried to hit her? What if she hit her back? She was nervous and fidgety and she could not figure out what to do with her hands. They kept finding their way to her face, her chest, until at last she grabbed one with the other and placed them both in her lap.

Lula took a good look at the woman who sat across

from her. Miss Martha had lost weight. She looked pale and old. Much older than her fifty-four years. Her skin sagged with age and Lula could see the old woman's veins.

"I haven't seen much of you lately," Mrs. Fleming started. "How have you been doing?"

"I'm all right. Work every day. Eat every day."

Martha Fleming folded her thin fingers together. "Well those are good things indeed, but do you ever want more than that?"

"No, Ma'am. What more is there?"

"Lots of things. Why, there's music and art and travel." She picked up her cup from its saucer and took a sip of her tea. Then she leaned forward to look into Lula's eyes. "Have you ever thought about having your own home?"

"No, Ma'am."

"I think it is time you do. I've noticed something about you. You do as much work around here as the men and twice as much as the women. You never complain and you don't talk back. You don't have any children to take care of. Somehow it does not seem right for you to work so hard and then come home to the quarters filled with a bunch of cackling hens and squalling babies. I want you to have your own place. There is a little spot down by the pond. Now, it's not much, but it sits on about an acre of land, so you could have your own garden. There is a path that leads to the pond. You could fish every day."

Mrs. Fleming clapped her hands and giggled like a school girl.

"Are you talking about the cabin I was born in?"

"Oh, so you know about it. Have you ever been there?"

"Yes, Ma'am. Susan took me there when I was a little girl."

"Well, I want you to have it. It'll be your own private place and nobody can go in there unless you say so. You will have to clean it up a bit because it's been empty since your mother died, but it's yours as long as you want it. I put that in my will. Nobody will ever be able to take it from you. Mind you, I am not bequeathing it to you; more like *assigning* you the responsibility of it is what I'm doing.

I know you will take good care of that piece of property. And like I said, you can stay there as long as you live."

"I don't know what to say, Miss Martha."

"The polite thing to say is 'Thank you.'"

"I surely thank you. Thank you, Miss Martha."

Martha rose and so did Lula. It was a sign that the conversation was complete and Lula was being dismissed. In that moment the two women shared a rare intimacy that the younger woman could not define. A deepness in the older woman's eyes and the tremble around her lips, suggested that she had feelings for Lula that were beyond definition. A hug might have been appropriate, but neither of them chose to make such an awkward move.

"Be happy, my dear." It was the last thing Mrs. Fleming said to Lula Cooper.

Martha Fleming died a few weeks later. She left most of her land and all her money to charity. The only thing she left to Mr. Fleming was the job he already held. He was to be paid a salary as long as he lived there. And, true to her word, she left Lula with a lifetime lease on her cabin.

For the next few years Lula lived her life simply, working hard every day and relaxing in her cabin at night. The big house that was on the property burned to the ground in 1858, shortly after Martha died. Only the chimney and the steps remained. Chinaberry trees sprouted and grew over the ground, but Lula made a path that led to her cabin. She felt a connection to that house. She didn't love it; she just felt bound to it. The little information she knew about her own history created a strong affinity to the house, so she wanted to make sure she could always access it.

She used a sickle to cut her grass down to the root. With the pond so close, snakes could easily hide in tall grass. Her place was like an oasis at the end of the dark and dense woods, and once in a while a traveler would mount her steps out of curiosity. Lula was always polite and accommodating—some fried fish and lemonade, maybe. Depending on his appearance, he might even become fortunate enough to spend the night, but then she would send him on his way in the morning.

Hearing about her lifestyle, Jim hinted that he wanted a repeat performance.

"Can I come to see you sometime?" he asked.

"Aww…no thanks."

"Here you got that fine house and you live there by yourself. Ain't you scared?"

"No."

"Well, don't you get lonely sometimes?"

"Not at all."

He shrugged his shoulders and looked down at his feet. After a moment, he looked up to meet her eyes. "I can be good for you, Lula. I can help you."

"Help me do what?"

"Anything. Chop wood. Cut the grass. Make sure you get what you need…at night, you know."

"I can chop wood and cut grass. And whatever I need at night is none of your business."

She watched the smile slowly fade from his face and eyes. He knotted his brows. And when he reached out to touch her arm she said, "Get away from me with that little bitty dick."

He looked like he had been slapped in the face. "You a cold, cold woman, Lula."

"I was born in a blizzard. What do you expect?"

●

Toisnot was a small community that formed around the Toisnot Primitive Baptist Church in the early 1800s. It was primarily a wooded area that touched the borders of four counties: Edgecomb, Nash, Johnston and Wayne. With the advent of the railroad in 1839 the area became a major attraction for people who sought to own land, establish businesses and accumulate wealth. Most noteworthy of these new residents was Louis D. Wilson. He was an important figure in that he was active in the

State Senate and, like Mr. Cooper, he was a faithful and loyal member of the U. S. Volunteers. Indeed, he was very popular with the ladies as he was known widely for his bravery. He organized two regiments of militia and set off to fight in the Mexican-American War while he was on leave from the Senate. On the trail he contacted yellow fever and died in 1848. But he was a hero of the people, so they named the town after him, and on January 29, 1849, the North Carolina General Assembly chartered Wilson, North Carolina.

Lula loved to go to Wilson. She had a dog named Susu and a horse named Sally. They were her companions when she visited Wilson on Saturday afternoons. That was the place where she wanted to live out her days. It was a growing little area, with plenty of work and plenty of tall, black men. Many of the slaves on the Cooper Plantation were allowed to earn money—real money—by being hired out to perform tasks such as cutting down trees, killing snakes or doing laundry. They worked the stables, served as delivery boys and ran errands business to business. Sometimes they were paid in cowrie beads, a method of trade left over from the Tuscarorans who used to dominate that area and named it Toisnot. And since few ever had the opportunity to go into town and shop, the beads were favored among the slaves. Lula had a huge collection of cowries as a result of her healing prowess. She decided to save all her money, and if freedom should come within her lifetime, she would buy a little spot in Wilson and stay there until death took her.

Whenever she took that trip, Susu ran ahead to warn her of potential danger. Lula was, after all, over six feet tall and could, therefore, be perceived as a threat to a fellow traveler. But Lula walked alongside of Sally. She did not think it was right to ride her, or to burden any animal with the weight of a human being.

She only stayed long enough to get the feel of Wilson, the smell of it. The whistle of the train and the clickety clack of hammer on nail excited her beyond compare.

Wilson promised growth, the future, and the absolute promise of a brighter day. In the evenings she could hear the music from the juke joints way down deep into the woods. She smelled the aroma of fried fish and she heard the laughter of the people who relaxed there after a hard day's work. And while she had the urge to go down there, she never surrendered. She was not yet ready, she thought, and she did not want to alter her plans. So, instead, she and Susu and Sally would turn around and start the eighteen-mile trek back home where she could soak her feet in a hot tub of sudsy, salted water and get ready for work on Monday. Regardless of the state of Wilson, the nation, the *planet* even, she saw herself as absolutely free.

Her freedom became real in 1863 when President Lincoln issued the Emancipation Proclamation. Mr. Fleming gathered them all to make the announcement. There was pain in his face.

"Y'all are welcome to stay here as long as you want to. Nothing will change, but everything has changed. Right now, you are as free as I am if that means anything to you. It won't be much, but you will be paid for the work you do around here. Just like me. You can stay, or you can go. Up to you." He took out his handkerchief and wiped his nose.

●

Most of the workers did stay. They had heard stories about white men who hunted and killed free blacks even before emancipation. They felt safety in the umbrella of protection that the Cooper Plantation provided. They worked together, lived together, ate together, and raised their children together.

And then one day in 1866 Louie, one of Mazzie's boys, told them that colored troops were forming all across the state and he was planning to leave and join one of them.

Lula made plans to entertain the colored troops and relieve them of their stress. She believed she could handle an entire regiment if they would just come her way. She developed a fantasy about the whole scene, and she nurtured it in every way possible. She often dreamed about the young men coming to her with sweat on their brows and mud on their boots. She climbed her favorite hill to search the horizon, everyday anticipating their arrival.

It never happened, of course, because the closest the troops came was New Bern and, aside from the fact that it was much too far to walk, her pride would not let her go to them.

Slavery was over and Lula was comfortable, settled, at least for now. She and everyone else who worked the land were paid small salaries, just like Mr. Fleming had said, and with a house that was paid for, a garden full of fresh vegetables and a pond loaded with fresh water bass, Lula saved almost every dime she earned.

With all this in mind, Lula never jumped the broom. She didn't have to. She worked right alongside the men. From her teenage years to grown womanhood, whenever she felt the need to be with a man that way, she'd choose one and they would drop where they were. She rejected all notions of permanency. The excitement of the first kiss was her motivation for choosing a new man every time. She hated the white blood in her, and she chose her lovers carefully. They all had to be blue-black, with ashy ankles and crusty knees. And to make sure she did not conceive any children, she cut a lemon in half crosswise, took out the pulp and used the remains as a diaphragm. It was a very successful contraceptive and one that was readily available. Her reputation as a good lay grew, and she was eager to oblige, never disappointing, and always, *always* prepared.

Except once.

"It's your turn, gal," was all he said when the foreman caught her at the edge of the tobacco field. She tried to sweet talk him, begging him to let her wash off the sticky fluid that collects on the hands when one crops tobacco leaves. But he was determined to take her right there in front of God and everybody. Of course, no one did anything to stop it. The rest of the workers looked on in amusement as Mr. Grimes satisfied his needs. They covered their mouths to keep from laughing out loud at the whiteness of his ass there in the sunshine, his pants to his knees, his boots digging in the ground. When he finished, he left Lula in the dirt. Her legs wide open, her eyes wet with humiliation, and a seed in her belly that would not be washed away.

So, when her daughter was born in 1871, Lula gave the child her name: Lula Cooper. But she added a "B" to make things easier for folks to address them separately. Eventually the name would seemingly shorten itself, and folks just called the child "Bee."

Bee Cooper was to become the object of her mother's hatred. Lula had said that she did not want children because she believed she lacked the emotional strength it took to raise a child properly. Her predictions about herself turned out to be true. This child got in her way—disturbed her pattern of living life after her own fashion. Aside from the fact that Bee was a quadroon and covered in a creamy, squash-colored skin, she was conceived without permission.

Lula mothered Bee with the same care she would give to a stray cat. She saw to it that the child was clean and fed. She tried to teach her responsibility by letting her collect the eggs from the henhouse. She even let her sell them for three cents each, and she allowed Bee to keep the money. Beyond that there was nothing. Bee was simply a reminder of her weakness on the day Mr. Grimes robbed her of the only thing that was truly her own.

At campfire singings grownups spoke in softened tones to protect themselves and their children. They told stories of lynching and stories of triumph. The children found their mothers who, in turn, placed their hands over the children's ears and settled them on their laps for comfort and protection. Seeing this, Bee walked over to Lula and attempted to lie on her. "Get away from me,"

Lula said. "Go find something else to do."

Susan cut her eye sharply towards Lula who rolled her eyes and turned her head. She would never disrespect Susan, after all, she owed her own life to Susan. But even Susan could not make her love a child she never asked for and did not want. Bee had disrupted her life and demanded more attention than Lula was willing to give.

One day when Bee was seven, she went running through the fields. She cut her foot on a rusted tin can. Lula rushed to her side, cleaned and patched the wound, and then she spanked the child for being clumsy.

Susan felt the need to speak to Lula about her distance towards Bee.

"That girl needs your love," Susan told her.

"She has to learn how to love herself," replied Lula.

"Why are you so mean to her? What did she ever do to you?"

Lula looked at her daughter with contempt. "She was born."

Three

As months rolled into years Susan kept close watch on Lula and her daughter. She believed that she was the only one who could protect the child from her non-caring mother. Lord knows she had tried her best to show Lula how to love and be loved. Lord *knows* she tried, but it didn't take. Lula was as distant to her daughter as Susan was to all those babies she got but did not bear. Only now did Susan start to regret getting rid of those children. Here, in her golden years, she wondered what kind of lives they might have had. Would they sing or dance? Would they have a trade like carpentry or sewing? Indeed, how many of them were sons and how many were daughters? Surely, she could have been a real grandma by now—maybe even a great grandma. But the thought of having babies by strange men was repulsive to her. Mr. Fleming kept trying to breed her like an animal, but she fought his every effort. Since all those young bucks had sired dozens of children, Mr. Fleming was sure that the problem lay with her. He was so *stupid.* It took all her strength to not laugh in his face when he said to her, "Well, Susan, I guess you just barren."

And she said, "Yes, Sir. I reckon so, Sir."

Susan had been at the Cooper plantation all her life. Eighty-four years. She was born there. Her mother had squatted in a field of green tobacco, pushed her out, tied Susan onto her chest with a piece of hopsack and resumed her work. When she returned to quarters in the evening, she spoke with Clara, the cook.

"I can work faster and harder if you are willing to watch this child for me during the day."

"I can watch her at night, too, so you can rest," Clara said. As simple as that, Clara became Susan's adopted mother.

Abby worked herself into an early grave. Once in a while she would sneak into the backyard and visit with Susan. Each time Abby would tell her daughter stories about their homeland, Senegal. She once shared with Susan the miracle of her birth—how Abby was captured and sent to Gorée Island:

We were an important part of Senegalese culture. We were griots or grewels as we pronounce it in Wolof. It was our job to perform ceremonies at weddings and funerals, to announce the birthing of babies and to pass on folklore from generation to generation. My mother taught me as her mother taught her. We had a good life—full of love, food and plenty of sunshine. On the day that I was captured my mother and I were digging yams. I will never forget it. We were on our hands and knees when a band of armed men charged at us. My mother told me to run. I did, but I ran right into the hands of another one. I could see my mother struggling and fighting her captor. He hit her with the butt end of his gun and she went down. I started screaming and the man who held me had my arms twisted behind me. I was only fourteen years old, "ma chèrie", and just a few months married. I did not know where my husband was.

There were about a hundred of us taken that day. They put us all in chains and shackles and made us walk for many hours. It got dark. Then they put us on a long, flat boat and took us to Gorée Island. There was a huge house that they kept us all in and they separated the men from the women and the women from their children. They took our clothes. There was sickness and even death in that big house. I remember it had a big, open door that looked out onto the sea. We called this door "la porte de non retour." It led to a very large boat. The house sat on a hill of volcanic rock. One by one the men unchained us and made us walk through that door. I could hear grown men crying. Some of them refused to go on the boat, so they were thrown onto the rocks below. I begged Allah to take me that day, but after seeing what happened to those who resisted, I chose to go with the men rather than die on the rocks.

We traveled for months in the belly of the boat. The women were still separated from the men, but we were chained together. I never did see my mother again. Nor my husband. It was cold and the boat rocked from side to side. With you growing in my belly, I had a hard time keeping the little food they allowed us.

After a long while the boat stopped rocking. We were led out of the boat still chained to one another. There we would have the most un-Godly experience. We were positioned on a block and white men were allowed to gaze at us, argue over us. They checked our hair and our teeth. They felt between my legs. They shouted words we did not understand. And then most of us were thrown onto the back of a wagon and sent to different places where we would be immediately put to work.

Monsieur Cooper bought me and, seeing my condition, he put a coat over me to hide my nakedness. Alhamdulillah! I went to work in the fields and soon after I got here you were born. I have been out there in those fields ever since, but Monsieur Cooper wanted you to learn how to cook and keep house. He and his wife had a little baby girl, Miss Martha, and it looked like he wanted you to be her companion. He used to let you play together. But it was always clear that Clara was supposed to train you so they would have somebody to prepare the food in case she died or something. I want you to know that I loved your Papa and I love you. But this is no kind of life. The whites will take a child from its mother as easy as they would take a pup from a bitch dog. If I had known this was going to happen, I would not have gotten you. But I promise you, you are the best thing that ever happened to me. Masha Allah. Fi Amanillah.

•

Susan started cooking in the big house when she was seven. Clara taught her very little; cooking was a natural gift to her. Abby had taught her how to make *thieboudienne*, and since the pond was always full of fish, she made it for herself often. She and Martha Cooper were the same age and, if it were not for the fact that Martha was white and Susan was colored, one might have called them sisterly friends. Susan was Martha's company, especially in the evenings of winter when the sun went down long before bedtime. She was Martha's confidante as a teenager and her *special* caregiver; it was Susan who hand washed Martha's undergarments when she accidentally soiled them overnight. They had an energy that never flagged. Martha told Susan all her secrets and the latter listened patiently, intently, even though she did not understand half of them. When Martha met Flannigan Fleming, Susan was the first to know. Martha knew her secrets were safe, even from her own mother. She always treated Susan and the rest of the slaves with kindness, as her father had instructed her to do. She once heard him speaking with an overseer. He said, "There are only three rules on this plantation: You don't mess with my daughter, you don't kick my dog, and you do *not* whip my slaves. I paid good money for them. So, if one of them gets out of line, you let me know and I will handle it. Understand?"

That was the way it was then. But times were changing. It was now 1886. With slavery *and* Martha gone, some of the folks in their little community had taken to the North to find work, peace, and happiness. Those who remained, however, still held onto the slave mentality. They did as they were told, but they harbored secrets among themselves that they generally shared with each other and kept from the whites. It was a rule they all took for granted, and anyone who broke that rule became an outcast in their eyes.

That form of treachery was not tolerated at all, and the traitor was never again allowed to participate in campfire celebrations or to have privy to any further secrets. In fact, if that person walked into a discussion about a serious issue the subject was immediately changed to something nontoxic, like the weather.

One such person was Gerty. She had a demonstrated history that disallowed the working community to trust her. She was new to the plantation nearly sixty years ago when she set her sights on Benny. Gerty was a fast woman. She had no shame in her pursuit of Benny. She followed him everywhere. She would leave the fields in search of him. Perhaps it was his coolness towards her that fueled her desire for him. No one ever knew what the attraction was, but Gerty could often be seen hiding behind a tree as she spied on Benny.

Susan was standing at the stove when Gerty rushed into the kitchen one day. She looked crazed. Her eyes were stretched wide and she slobbered profusely.

"Susan! Susan!"

Susan wiped her hands on a towel and handed it to Gerty. "What's the matter, child?"

"Benny...Benny...he...he down at the barn."

"That's where he works."

"He down there...with...Miss *Martha!*"

"Oh." Susan laughed. "Is that all? I know that. She took him some lemonade."

"It ain't lemonade that he's tasting!"

"What do you mean?"

"I mean he's down there *with* Miss Martha! They...they doing it!"

"Shut your mouth!"

"But I saw them."

"I said shut your mouth. You ain't seen nothing. You hear me? You ain't seen nothing!"

Gerty continued to protest until Susan placed her hand over Gerty's mouth.

"Now you listen to me. You go on back to work and

forget what you think you saw. Don't you ever speak on it again. You hear?"

"Yes, Ma'am. But I know what I saw. I ain't crazy. No wonder he don't want no parts of me. He down there with *her*. I saw them. Miss Martha looked right at me. She know I want Benny. You need to tell Mr. Fleming." Gerty suddenly became very smug and completely composed. "If you don't...I *will!*"

Shortly after that Benny disappeared. Nobody could find him anywhere. Susan suspected that Gerty had kept her word. After all, she did become Mr. Fleming's concubine for a short while. Her tenure as Mr. Fleming's *cunt* caused her to feel superior to all the other women. She was nasty to them and she often threatened to tell Mr. Fleming if she caught one of them stealing supplies.

This went on for several years and the hatred for Gerty mounted. She did not belong there. She was an outsider from the first day of her arrival. The women hated the way she strutted about as if the plantation belonged to her. They talked about her behind her back at campfire. This intensified the hatred and, ultimately, sealed her fate.

"What y'all reckon? Miss Gerty think she better than us?"

"That's what I figure."

"She just ain't got no shame is all. She makes googley eyes at Mr. Fleming right in front of us."

"He do too! You noticed that? I thought I was the only one."

"Naw, everybody sees that. Even the men. And they don't like it. It's like she telling them that they ain't good enough for her."

"Maybe they ain't. If they had any sense they wouldn't even want her. After what happened to Benny—"

"Hush yo' mouth!"

"Well it's the truth. A man don't just up and disappear in thin air like that. Y'all know Mr. Fleming did something to him. Gerty the one that caused it. Everybody knows that."

"Yeah. But what we gon' do? She got old man Fleming wrapped around her little finger."

"That may be the way it is now, but it don't have to be

that way. Maybe we can do some unwrapping."

"What you mean?"

"I mean, we need to teach her a lesson."

"Well I'll help you whip her if you want me to."

"Gonna take more than a whippin.' Some of you tried that and look what happened. Look what happened to Jane. When Gerty and Jane fought Mr. Fleming made Jane take all her children and leave the plantation."

"So...what can we do?"

"We can fix it so he don't want her no more. That's what we can do."

"How we gon' do that?"

"You'll see soon enough. She is a danger to all of us here. She has to be stopped."

Just about that time Gerty came into the yard and the talking ceased. "What you biddies doing out here?"

One of the women replied, "Oh nothing. Just talking about frying some fish out here tomorrow night is all."

They all looked at each other and winked. If there was one thing Gerty liked it was fried bass fresh out of the pond. She was too lazy to cook them for herself, so she always managed to be around when someone else was doing the cooking.

The women all fished the pond the next day. In the evening they gathered to clean their catch and they built a fire. It was a beautiful, clear night. The moon was bright and the stars sprinkled the sky like freckles. They made slaw and lemonade and hush puppies. When the first batch of fish hit the hot grease, the aroma traveled for miles. Just about time they were done, in walked Gerty. She grabbed a tin plate.

"I been waiting for this all day!" she said.

Susan said, "We plan to feed the children first. Have a seat."

"Looks like you got plenty. Them young'uns can wait. I'm hungry now!" She stuck out her hand to grab a piece of fish. Suki slapped her hand away.

"You hard of hearing? She *said*...we are going to feed

the children *first.* Sit yo' ass down and wait."

With that, Gerty hauled off and slapped Suki in the face. It seemed like all the women jumped on her at one time. The men stood around slack-jawed and watched as the women dragged Gerty away from the campfire. They punched and kicked her and shouted obscenities that the children had never heard. One of them used a scaling knife and she cut Gerty from the top of her forehead down through her eyebrow. The serrated blade went alongside her face and through her lower lip. They beat Gerty until they were too tired to eat. They left her face down and crying at the base of the chinaberry tree.

When the fight was over, the men fixed plates for the children and Gerty limped off to her cabin. No one saw her for several days. When she finally emerged, she went straight to Mr. Fleming. He was repulsed by what he saw. Both her eyes were black and bloodshot. The wound on her face was wide and filled with pus. Her lower lip hung slack on her chin.

"What happened to you?!"

Gerty opened her mouth to speak, but nothing intelligible came out. She babbled on and on, but after a while Mr. Fleming told her to be quiet.

"Go back to your cabin and fix yourself up."

•

For weeks Gerty walked with a limp. Her left eye remained closed and the left side of her mouth was constantly open. It never did heal right. The scar on her face was shaped like a crescent. Mr. Fleming couldn't stand to look at her anymore, so he told Gerty he was sending her to Wilson to be a maid for one of his cousins.

She cried and screamed and held on to his leg begging him to let her stay. The men and women gathered to watch the spectacle. Mr. Fleming dragged her through the dirt and practically threw her on the carriage.

Susan did not like what she saw. "It's my job to protect everyone around here," she said.

But the others were unimpressed with the scene. They were entertained. Suki said, "Oh don't go feeling sorry for her. She got what she deserved. Everything she got...she got with her ass. Now she gets to see how little that meant to him."

Rumor spread that Mr. Fleming starting violating the sheep on the property after that.

•

Now, Susan sat rocking on the front porch of her cabin. Lately she had taken to smoking a pipe, and as she watched the sunset, she reflected on her life at Cooper Plantation. Eighty-four years. The mourning doves had built a nest in the tree next to her porch. They seemed particularly mournful today. Their song, the fluttering of their wings, made tears come to her eyes. She thought of Maybelle and the way she willed herself to death. And Miss Martha. Martha Cooper Fleming had been the closest she had ever had to a best friend. They used to be so young, so full of energy and life. Now Martha was dead, and Susan was a tired and sick old woman. She had such awful memories. Awful memories. She could feel them in her chest, and she felt like they would come out on their own. The stories she could tell about Martha. About Benny. About Ed and Sam. And her mother. Her own mother, who dropped dead in the same field that Susan had been born in. And poor Annie. A child herself struggling to birth a baby that was almost as big as she was.

Susan had been the keeper of secrets her entire life. She was the healer of spirits, the one who presided at funerals, marriages and births. Her mission in life had been to protect, to honor, to glorify. She had failed old Gerty, but she saw it as her duty, a vindication, even. Her loyalty lay with Miss Martha.

The secrets overwhelmed her, filled her, and she felt the need to empty the burdens of them onto someone else. One day she would have to tell Lula the truth about poor Annie. Yes. That at least. She would have to tell Lula the truth about herself. One day.

Four

BEE WAS A REBEL FROM THE START. AS A BABY SHE SLEPT all day and stayed awake the whole night. As a child she refused to help with the daily chores. She seemingly saw it as beneath her. She would sit for hours combing her hair and admiring her image in the mirror. She loved being clean, and she often begged Lula to interrupt her schedule so that Bee could take a bath. On one occasion when Lula had company the man said to Bee, "You sure are a pretty little thing." And with the air of a grown woman Bee replied, "Yes. I know."

Over the years this would become a major issue between mother and daughter. They argued constantly about Bee's attitude, the womanish style of her hair, the sassy sling of her hips when she walked. If Lula's company did not comment on the child's beauty, Bee would bring it to his attention.

"Did you notice how pretty I am?"

The man, caught off guard, would stutter something like, "Why, yes. Yes, I did."

"I wonder where I got it?" She looked scornfully at her mother.

"Shame on you!" Lula hissed. "Go find something to do with yourself."

The man looked sheepishly at both of them.

As Bee entered adolescence, Lula became increasingly resentful of her daughter. She suspected that her visitors were more interested in Bee, and she found herself competing with the child for attention. It was never a real threat to her, however, because Bee showed no interest beyond the acknowledgement of her long curly hair, her light skin and her green eyes. It pleased Bee to think that men desired her, and she felt empowered by the thought that she was untouchable.

Lula, on the other hand, saw the child's arrogance and she attempted to correct it. At first, she used a peach tree switch, an instrument with divine authority. For a while this kind of chastising was effective. A peach tree whipping did exactly what it was supposed to do. Its targets—legs, arms, back and buttocks—grew welts that reminded Bee that her behavior was unacceptable. But as she got older, the switch stopped working. Bee would wipe her face and continue doing whatever she pleased. Lula took to using her hands. Instead of a whipping, Bee received a beating. Instead of correction, Bee received punishment. And in Lula's attempt to urge Bee towards the proper way to conduct herself, Bee became increasingly rebellious. A peach tree switch served to keep her in her child's place. But a hand-beating transcended Bee's little girl place and posited her into the realms of womanhood.

By the time Bee was fifteen she sought the company of white boys. None of the colored boys interested her; it was the white boys who received her flirtatious stares, her generous smiles. It was the white boys that Bee invited to meet her behind the shed or in the barn. There was a reason for her choice; Bee wanted to have children. Pretty children. She, herself, looked like a goddess; so many people had told her so. And she believed that she could give her own children the love she so desperately wanted.

Lula warned her daughter, "Nothing white is good for you. Not white sugar, not white flour, not white salt. And especially *not* white men." But Bee dismissed her mother's concerns and rejected her advice.

"Things are different now, Ma," she said. "Ain't no slavery no more. I can be with anybody I want to."

"Not if you plan to stay in this house, you can't."

Bee squared her shoulders. There was nothing to make her back down. "Then maybe it is time for me to leave this house."

"Girl, I'll knock you down!"

"Well, we gon' be two grown women fighting in here!"

"I don't think so. I'ma hit you and you gon' hit the floor!"

"Oh, we will see about that!"

Bee expected a slap at least, but there was nothing but a cold stare between them. The thought of hitting one's mother seemed to shock them both, but Lula, unrelenting, unforgiving, and unmoved stood her ground. She could not beg Bee to stay.

"All right Miss Priss. You go ahead. Ain't nobody stopping you. But you gon' learn...this is a hard, cold world. I guess you gon' have to learn that for yourself."

"I guess so."

Their words to each other were hard as bullets and, like bullets, there was no taking them back. The two women stared each other down until finally, Bee packed her things in a square of hopsack, tied it into a knot, and bolted out of her mother's house.

She walked rapidly for the first two miles. It was cool and clear that morning. After her anger subsided, she slowed her pace, trying to get her bearings and a sense of direction for Wilson. She headed to the General Store. Having saved her egg money, she had three dollars and sixty-seven cents. She could get to Wilson in about a day of hard walking. Beyond that, she had no plans. But she was pretty, high yellow and fifteen years old. She had reddish brown hair that kinked at the top and lay on her face around the edges, and she had green eyes. Somebody would be more than willing to take care of her. Of this she was certain.

•

Days folded into weeks as Lula waited for Bee to return. But nothing. Not even a word. Lula felt a sensation she had never known. She actually missed Bee. The thought of her daughter clouded her brain as she noticed every little thing. The awful silence. The echo in her empty house. The open jar of pomade that Bee had used on her hair. The leftover food. The lack of companionship. She missed that the most. Even when they argued they were in it together. Now Lula felt disconnected from the world. She kept going to the window. She frequently stepped onto the front porch and looked down the road, stretching her neck so she could see farther. She could not think clearly, wondering what was happening to Bee. Did she get where she wanted to go? Was she all right? Why had she not heard from her?

Alone in her cabin the walls seemed to close in on Lula. She couldn't breathe. She needed air, and she needed to talk with someone about this new feeling. She needed a woman's advice.

She went to see Susan.

Lula stood knocking on the door to Susan's cabin for what seemed like an eternity. Finally, she heard a voice so faint she hardly recognized it as the woman who had raised her.

"Who is it?"

"It's Lula, Susan. Are you all right?"

"Come on in. Door's unlocked."

Lula was dismayed by the sight that greeted her. The room was dark and dank. Dirty dishes cluttered the table and the floor. The smell of sickness penetrated her nostrils. Susan lay flat on her back.

"You sick? Why didn't you send for me?"

"Who I'm gon' send? Nobody comes here."

"Well, what's the matter?"

"I don't know. Got these pains in my belly and they cut off my breath when I try to sit up."

Lula reached for a pillow. "Here, let me help you."

She propped up Susan's head and started to walk away. Her immediate plan was to clean the cabin and cook something for her new patient.

Susan grabbed her arm. "Don't," she said. "Don't fuss. And don't leave me. Please. I don't want to die alone,"

So, Lula sat on the edge of the bed and stroked Susan's hair with her fingers.

"I heard that Bee left. You hear from her yet?"

"No."

"You care?"

"Not much. My daughter is a wild woman. She never listened to me."

"That's the reason she left."

"What are you talking about?"

"Your daughter. You could not see her as a person. Just your daughter. She had desires and needs like any other person. When the sap starts rising, you can't stop Mother Nature from doing her thing. Birds, bees, bugs... they all get it. Bee needed her some too, but you so busy trying to hold on to your *daughter,* you couldn't see the blooming young woman."

"You might be right."

"Lula...I...I got something to tell you."

"All right."

"Lord. I don't even know where to begin. I guess you heard about Miss Martha messing around with them colored boys."

"Yes ma'am, but that's been so long ago. Why you fretting about it now?"

"'Cause I have to tell you. It wasn't her fault. Mr. Fleming was never right for her. He didn't know what to do to keep her happy."

"I don't care nothing about them---" Lula tried to withdraw her arm, but Susan tightened her grip.

"No! Don't go. You have to listen, 'cause you have to know. Can you move them babies?"

"What babies?"

"Them babies crawling round my feet. Don't you see 'em? Their cords are binding my feet."

Lula realized that Susan was talking out of her head. "Okay, I'll get them. You rest now and I'll fix you something to eat."

"I ain't hungry, and I ain't got time to rest. My life has always been so hard. Guess I thought dying would be easier. I'm glad you come. I'm dying, Lula, and I got to tell you before I go."

"All right."

Susan wiped her mouth with the back of her hand. She looked hard at Lula and then she let her eyes wander. She seemed to be talking to the air.

"When Mr. Fleming got rid of Benny, nobody ever knew what happened to him. But everybody knew it was that damned Gerty who told it. She was terrible. She used to strut around the yard like a prize hen. Like she was better than us 'cause she was with Mr. Fleming. She would tell on folks just so she could see how loud they could holler when they got a whipping. Mr. Cooper never let anybody whip us, but after he died, Mr. Fleming and Mr. Donovan used the whip almost every day. They sent Mazzie's man to kill a hog one day. When he brought it back, cleaned and ready for the pit, Gerty told Mr. Fleming that the chit'lins were missing. He beat that ol' boy half to death.

"She had already told on Benny. Everybody knew it was her. They started to make plans to fix her good. The women all jumped on Gerty one night and beat the snot out of her. They cut her face with a scaling knife. Oh Lord...they cut her from the top of her forehead down through her mouth. It's a wonder she did not lose that eye. I don't know which one of the women did it, but she finished Gerty's strut right then and there. The knife cut her bottom lip half off. She never did heal neither. Uh uh. That eye stayed half closed and her lip laid on her chin. She couldn't close her mouth for shit. She looked like a mule had kicked her, or she had a stroke or something. It was awful."

Susan started to laugh a rolling grunt that made her eyes water. As she wiped them, she said, "She was so ugly, nobody could stand to look at her, not even Mr. Fleming. So he sent her away. Heh heh, she would have been pitiful if she wasn't so devilish mean. But I tell you what, she never told nothing on nobody again. I tell you that!"

Susan cleared her throat and raised herself up on an elbow.

"When Benny came up missing, Miss Martha took an interest in Ed. She made him her driver, and once in a while they would go off in the morning and stay all day. After a while, Miss Martha started to put on weight. She and Mr. Fleming hardly ever spent any time together, so he didn't even notice. But I did. And I also noticed that I didn't have to wash her cottons in vinegar—'bout three months as best as I could count. So, Miss Martha told me what was the matter, and she told Mr. Fleming that she was going away for a while. Said she always wanted to take a boat ride to England and France and other far-off places. Her husband never knew what was wrong with her, but he could not stop her from doing what she wanted to do. So, she set sail and, after she left, somebody told Mr. Fleming that Ed was her favorite slave. That made him think about Benny. So, he and Mr. Donovan told Ed to go hitch up the wagon 'cause they had to go to Snow Hill. They left early that morning, and when they came back that night—Mr. Fleming and Mr. Donovan—Ed was not with them. They gathered us all together and told us that they left Ed in Snow Hill to do some work. Like they had to explain anything to *us!*"

Susan went into a coughing fit and almost lost her breath. Lula rolled her over and patted her back. When she recovered, she continued her story.

"So, the next morning some of the children were playing on the hill. You know, by that old oak tree you used to love? They found Ed. He was in a hole, and he was dead. Nobody ever said anything, but I know Mr.

Fleming and Mr. Donovan had done it. They shoved a pole from his ass to his right shoulder. It popped out just below his right ear. Then they built a fire in the hole and slow roasted him. Like a hog!"

Susan burst into tears and started to cough again. This time she waved away Lula's efforts.

"I ain't through. About a year later Miss Martha come back. She looked good—thin and glowing like sunshine. She had this great big smile on her face, and she had a baby in her arms. A little colored girl. 'This is Annie,' she said. 'I bought her in Paris. Ah...*c'est la vie!*' she said. I never told a soul, never even told Miss Martha, but I knew Annie was Miss Martha's own child."

Lula pressed her hand to her heart. "My mother Annie?!"

"That's right. Miss Martha gave her to me to raise, but she always checked on her. She admired her from a distance so Mr. Fleming would never know the truth. Annie was dark brown like her daddy, but she had long, straight hair. Pretty thing. Big for her age. Anyway, when she was eleven, Mr. Fleming gave her to Mr. Donovan and she got big. Miss Martha found out and she tried to poison the old man. She put a little rat poison in his tea. He was sick for days, but he got over it. Poor Annie never got over nothing. She was sick the whole time she carried you. She kept complaining that you were so big you took her breath away. Kept trying to push you down from under her heart. Then, on the night you were born, it was snowing so hard. She had been in labor for three days. You were coming feet first. The child couldn't take all that pain. So she died. I want you to know, Lula. Your mama didn't die on purpose. Wasn't trying to be mean to you. She died because it was easier than bringing you into the world."

Susan shuffled and kicked her feet as if she were trying to remove something.

"Are you telling me that Miss Martha was my grandma and that old stinking, vicious, drunken Mr. Donovan is my daddy?"

"That's what I'm telling you, girl."

"Oh my God! Oh my God oh my God oh my God!"

"That's the reason Miss Martha give you that land. She believed she owed you something. And she wanted to make sure nobody could ever take it from you."

Lula stood up and paced the floor. She always knew there was something about Miss Martha that seemed familiar. Never in her wildest thoughts did she think of this.

"Come back over here," Susan pleaded. "Come help me get rid of these babies. Look. Can't you see 'em? They tying knots around my feet. It's so hot in here. Help me, Lula. Help me get rid of them. Oh Lord, it's so *hot.* Get these babies from around my feet!"

Susan's body stretched out stiff as plywood. She threw her hands over her head and with a deep, gut-wrenching yell, she left this world.

"No...wait," Lula said.

But Susan was dead. Anybody could see that. Lula started towards her and then stopped and retraced her steps backward. Her eyes darted to spots in that little room: the dirty dishes, the damp walls, the dead woman in that bed. The woman who for all purposes had been her mother. At once she felt both empty and full. The air was still and thick. Stifling. She thought her chest would burst open. She charged through the door and went running through the woods. The animals in the forest got out of her way. She ducked low branches and dodged snakes, and she kept on running. It was only when she reached the edge of the pond that she realized she had been screaming all the way. And for the second time in her whole life, Lula sat right down in the dirt and cried.

Five

The new owners of the Cooper property started to clear the land. More than thirty years had passed since Martha's death and just as the place began to look like a wilderness, teams of horses and plows and men came in and knocked down pine trees and hauled away debris. Eventually, they cut roads and streets, and the owners sold off portions to folks who built homes there. It was very fertile soil—good for gardening and good, still, for planting tobacco, cotton and corn. Most people bought five- or ten-acre tracts and dug out their own wells. There was an occasional herd of cows or sheep, one chicken farm, a hog island—made so when the owner carved his own pond all around his acreage. The largest piece belonged to a man who raised horses. His place was across the pond from Lula. She could see him, and he could see her. Once in a while they would share a wave, but neither of them ever bothered the other.

Years ago, Lula had placed a tin chair on the bank so she could sit and fish. Lately, though, she just sat and thought. She'd go to the bank when the sun was high, raise her face to receive the warmth, and sit there for hours, musing. It was her *escape* from the ordinary, the mundane, the *busyness* of a growing area. She never slept there, but she went into a kind of meditative trance that made her all but oblivious to her surroundings. She thought of her real mother, Annie, and how scared she must have been. So young. Too young to take on the burdens of the world. She thought of Susan, strong and strong handed. Nurturing. And she thought of Miss Martha, her grandmother. She tried to focus on her own daughter, Bee, but the image of her now just would not come. It was 1888, and Bee had been gone for two years. Lula had not heard a word from her in all that time.

On one of these escape days Lula was shelling peas when she heard a voice that sounded like it was coming from within her. It sounded far away, almost as if coming through a tunnel. A man's voice that seemed to rise like a crescendo in its urgency. It startled her so badly she slipped off the edge of her chair and fell much too close to the water.

"Ma'am...Ma'am..." the voice said.

Lula got to her knees and turned to see a very tall, dark-skinned man leading a horse.

"Excuse me, Ma'am," he said. "I didn't mean to scare you."

"You didn't scare me. I just wasn't expecting company is all."

"I hate to admit it, but I am lost. I'm looking for Barnes Stables. Do you know of any place like that around here?"

"I don't know the name." She thought for a second and quickly added, "But there is a horse farm right there." She pointed across the pond. "You can see it from here. Maybe that's what you looking for."

He followed the direction of her finger. "Oh. Why thank you, Ma'am."

"If you keep going that way past my house, there is a bridge about a hundred yards down. It'll take you right over there."

"Yes, Ma'am. I thank you."

Lula watched him mount his horse and leave. She tried to go back to her thoughts, but the spell was broken. So she walked the short distance back to her house.

A few days later the man returned. Lula was sitting on the porch peeling potatoes.

"I brought you a present," he said. "To show my appreciation."

"Oh, you didn't have to do that. I'm glad I could help."

She took the gift and opened it. It was a bottle of rose water. No man had ever given her a present. No one except Miss Martha had ever given her anything, and she didn't quite know how to behave. But she was acutely aware of the broad grin on her face. She felt awkward, clumsy. Was this man trying to court her? There was only one way to find out.

"Thank you," she said as she remembered Miss Martha's instructions. "I was just about to throw these potatoes into some water, but the fish and cornbread are already done. Would you like to come in for a mouthful?"

He parted his lips to reveal a set of perfect, gleaming white teeth. "Well," he said. "Don't mind if I do."

His name was Foots Walker, and he was a singing man. He pulled out a harmonica and played and sang while Lula finished cooking. Years ago, she had stopped bedding down every man she met. She secretly blamed her behavior as one of the reasons Bee had left. Besides, she was well past forty almost fifty, even, and men were no longer easy for her to get. They liked those young girls who didn't have a nickel's worth of sense in their heads. But sense wasn't what they sought.

After supper they sat on the porch and watched the sun slip quietly into the night. Foots played his harmonica and Lula danced to his music. That was the best she had ever felt in her entire life. The joy of it. The purity. The absolute freedom to be herself with a man who required nothing of her. They talked until the mosquitoes threatened to eat them alive and, as he left, he asked if he could come back again.

"I'm here every day," she smiled.

Over the next few weeks Lula and Foots grew more and more fond of each other's company. Sometimes when she fished, she would see him across the pond. They waved to one another briefly, a wave that assured them both that they would be together in the evening. Occasionally, he would come a little early and take a swim. Of all her gifts, and all her talents, Lula never learned how to swim, but she thoroughly enjoyed watching him splash in the water. He offered to teach her how, but truth be told, Lula was a bit skittish of water. When she was a child, she caught a rag on her hook. After examining it she realized that it was a part of an old shirt. Her imagination ran wild, and she convinced herself that the owner of the shirt must be dead in that pond. So, she stayed out of the water and Foots swam alone. Afterwards they would eat supper and drink whiskey. And Lula, a gifted dancer, glorified the music he made.

"Where do you sleep over there?" she asked him one evening.

"I sleep in the stables."

"With the horses?" Her face twisted in disbelief.

He laughed. "Look at your face. It ain't so bad."

Maybe it was the whiskey that made her say what she did. Maybe it was the whiskey that gave her that warm feeling of contentment. She said to him, "I have a real bed with a real mattress. Why don't you spend the night?"

He said, "Okay."

They made love, and when morning came, he awoke to find her fishing for his breakfast. They fell into a pattern almost like a married couple. Almost. He would go to work all day and come home to her in the evenings. Lula danced happily every night. They were at one with nature: the birds chirping, the frogs croaking and the crickets thrumming. It was a symphony all her own. The moon and the stars all lined up in celebration of her. She felt empowered, protected, and happily involved. She had no need for any other; he satisfied her.

She found herself doing things to please him. He loved banana pudding, so she made it once a week. He liked to see a skirt swishing round her legs, so when she finished her day's work, she would bathe, splash herself with the rose water, and put on a clean dress. She felt a comfort she had never known, and she was at ease with calling him her *man.*

One evening she left her garden and ran home to beat an oncoming storm. The sky was dark grey, and the clouds moved in a rolling motion. She could see lightning in the distance, hear the frightful thunder, and she watched the birds twitter about as they sought shelter. The rain started just as Foots came racing to her porch. They stopped for a minute and looked at the steel grey sky; the drops of water were as large as marbles. The rain brought with it a cold, hard wind that whistled and groaned, and caused the rain to beat a rhythm on the tin roof. It aroused them both. They went to bed without supper, and they loved hard until they were both exhausted. She felt relaxed, as light as air. And without warning to her or him, she said something she had never said to anyone. She had never even thought it, but the words slipped out with such ease and such quality and such bare truth that it caused her to suck in her breath as she rolled over and went to sleep. "I love you," she said.

She slept soundly, and when she awoke the next morning, his spot on the bed was empty. The rain had stopped. Lula went to the front of her house and opened the screen door. His tracks were left in the mud. For days she looked across the pond hoping to get sight of him, but just as easily as he had walked into her life—just like that, he was gone. Lula felt a sickness in the pit of her stomach. She heaved, and when she finished vomiting, she sat down and tried to think of what she could have done wrong. She had planned to tell him that a baby was coming—just never quite got around to it. Now she would not want him to know anyway. The last thing she wanted was to have him come back out of a sense of duty. She burned the sheets they had slept on.

But then the irony of his name dawned on her: Foots Walker. Was it his real name? Was any of it real? Well, he had walked into her life, and he walked out. She would have to raise his seed alone, just like she did with Lula B.

The only difference was that Lula was not in the baby-making age. She was a forty-seven-year-old woman. By the time the child grew up Lula would be well past.... "Well," she said to herself. "No point in worrying about that now."

When Susan died, a part of Lula went with her. Foots had resurrected Lula. He taught her to love, to care for someone other than herself. Perhaps that was his purpose, to show her that life without love is not living; it is simply existing. Or maybe the reason was that since she was not good with Bee, God was giving her another chance. She committed to giving this child all the love she had. In that way, when Foots came back, and he would, she knew in her heart that he would, she could present him with a healthy, beautiful child. He needed to know that Lula was an effective, competent and attentive parent. He would need to know that Lula was capable of raising his seed.

•

Pearl was born in the spring of 1889—a perfect child. She was obedient and giving, and in spite of Lula's resistance to attachment, she came to realize that she actually did love Pearl. Because she had loved Foots so deeply, it did not even surprise her that she loved his child. Somehow Foots had anchored Lula and made her feel connected to something special.

Pearl looked like Lula. They shared a mutual respect for each other. They had no secrets between them, and they slept in the same bed until Pearl was five. Lula had long since forfeited her dream to move to Wilson. Instead, she added a room to her house for Pearl. Her daughter needed the security of a stable home. Their little community was still intact; the old farm workers had become like family. Lula had no worries about her daughter's safety, but she felt every growing up pain that Pearl experienced—a skinned knee, a bad tooth, even a headache. She coddled the child until Pearl was almost hopeless on her own. They were together every minute of the day and night. At last, Lula knew what it meant to love someone who could return the favor. Pearl was her special gift from God, sent late, but a gift, nonetheless. She was a little slow to learn things, and slow to react. Lula primped the child as best she could, stood wringing her hands over her when she was sick, spoon fed her until she was almost nine. She taught the girl how to cook and sew, to hunt and fish for food, to grow vegetables. She taught her how to keep herself and her house clean. She even tried to teach her about men, but that was something Lula did not know herself.

"The world is eager to make you feel less than others. Take care of your body and your house and everything else will fall in place. Outsiders only see you as a pound of meat. It's up to you to determine whether you want to be seen as a pound of hamburger or a pound of steak."

Lula walked to school with Pearl, and she was there to pick her up. Every day. They often took long walks together around the neighborhood, and when Lula started visiting with some of the women close by, she would take Pearl with her and let Pearl play with the neighbor's children. She never went inside their houses, however. She insisted on sitting on the porch where she could keep an eye on Pearl.

One of the neighbors had a new baby, so Lula made a peach cobbler and took it to her. This time she did go inside, accompanied by Pearl. It was the first time Pearl had seen a baby and they all *ooohed* and *ahhhed* over the size of his feet and hands. As they walked home Pearl asked Lula, "Where do babies come from Mama?"

"Do you really want to know?"

"Yes, Ma'am."

Even with Bee, Lula had maintained that if they are old enough to ask, they are old enough to know the truth. But this child was too young, too fragile. Lula didn't want to scare her.

"Well..." Lula started. "God gives the baby to the man, but he don't tote it. See, man is clumsy. He has to go to work, and he will be bumping into stuff. He could hurt the baby. So, he gives the baby to the woman to carry. Babies just love that squishy part of a woman's belly." She tickled Pearl's stomach, and the child squealed with laughter. "So, he puts the baby in the woman's belly, and it stays there until it is time to come out."

"How does it get out?"

Lula looked at her daughter's eyes. They were wide with curiosity and trust.

"Well, see, that's the really good part. Women have an opening that men don't have."

"Oh."

"You satisfied?"

"Yes, Ma'am."

"No more questions?"

"Yes, Ma'am."

"What?"

"That baby has a daddy. Did I ever have a daddy?"

"All babies have daddies."

"Where's mine?"

"He died before you were born."

"Oh. I wish that hadn't happened."

"So do I, Pearl. So do I."

When Pearl was about eight years old, Lula thought she saw Foots Walker across the pond. She waved, but the man did not wave back. It occurred to her that it might not be him, but if he ever came back, she would present his daughter proudly.

By now Mr. Fleming and Mr. Donovan were both long dead. The new residents of the community did not know them, so they were not missed. The neighborhood was growing fast. Houses jutted up like weeds. Children filled the front and backyards, a new school was built, and businesses developed rapidly as the neighborhood grew and prospered.

Pearl was very crafty. Her mother had taught her

to cook and sew, but Pearl taught herself how to make bracelets using cowrie beads. She sold them to the young girls in the area, and she saved all her money, except the money she spent on her Sunday afternoon sarsaparilla. But she saved the bottle caps, figuring that somehow, they could be useful one day.

On a cool morning in early October, Lula took the girl with her on her hunt. Pearl walked alongside her mother, and each step had a rattling sound to it. "What's that noise?" Lula asked.

"Oh, that's my bounty," laughed Pearl.

"Show me."

Pearl reached into her apron pocket and drew out the bag of bottle caps. She used her finger to rake through them and show her mother how many she had saved.

"What do you plan to do with them?"

"I don't know. Look to me like they were too pretty to just throw away, so I saved them."

"I can offer a suggestion that will be useful. Do you mind?"

"No, Ma'am."

Lula plucked two very stiff and sturdy switches from a nearby tree, and she handed one to Pearl. "Notice the size of it, now. About the width of my middle finger." Using her stick to demonstrate, she let Pearl work on her own. "You want to take all the leaves off of it. Understand?"

"Yes, Ma'am."

"Then square off one end like this." She used her knife to cut the end of the stick and make it even. "Then you want to make a point at the other end. Like this, see? You got your pliers with you?"

"Yes, Ma'am.

"Okay. Use your pliers to bend the cap over the sharp end. Now, take your pocketknife and cut a little groove in the flat end. Now you have a perfect arrow."

"What can I do with that?"

"Not much by itself. So now I am going to teach you how to make a bow. Then you can hunt quietly without alarming the other animals with a gunshot blast."

"Oh."

Lula looked around the forest until she found some dried bamboo sticks. "Here, help me pick up a couple dozen of these and let's go back to the house."

Once there, Lula sorted out fifteen of the sticks and she went to the tool shed for tape and string. They sat on the steps of the front porch and worked together. Hunting could wait until they had the proper tools. They could fish for their supper today.

Lula placed the bamboo sticks across her lap and let Pearl help her tape them together. Then she showed Pearl how to make a knot to string the new bow. Pearl was a natural at stuff like this. Once they had the first knot in place, Lula showed her how to string the other end and, therefore, bend the bow.

"You can kill animals as small as rabbits or as large as deer with this weapon. That way you will never be hungry."

Pearl thanked her mother and set about practicing on a tree where she had drawn a target. Before long she was hunting like an expert. In the next few years, the mother-daughter team lived harmoniously. Pearl would shoot rabbits and pheasants with her bow and arrows. Lula taught her how to dress them—skinning a rabbit was easier than plucking feathers from a bird, but Pearl learned quickly. There was nothing they wanted or needed, and life was good. Lula thought so at least.

Of course, Pearl was her mother's child, and it was not long before she started to feel a little too protected, a little too sheltered. As she matured, she became aware of the fact that her friends could come to see her, but she could not go to see them. She could not go anywhere alone. Couldn't do anything by herself. She had started her period at eleven, and that made things worse. Lula kept up with every month, marked the days on the calendar, and she could predict the hour that Pearl was supposed to start.

The only place Pearl went without a maternal chaperone was to church. Shortly after the turn of the century she met a boy there. They had an instant connection, and they took to meeting after Sunday school and before church services. They walked along the edges of the graveyard, and they sometimes sat on the outdoor baptismal pool to talk. He had big dreams about moving away.

"I have some people in Philadelphia," he told her. "They gon' help me find a job. I want you to come with me."

"Mama's never gon' let me go," she said.

"Why not? I can take good care of you."

"She gon' say I'm too young. Watch."

"You as much woman as any man will ever want or need."

They laughed together at that. "I want to be with you," she said. "But what can I do? I can't leave my mama all by herself."

"Sure, you can. Your mama's a tough old bird. She don't need nobody. She don't need a man, and she definitely don't need you."

"Maybe you right."

"'Course I am. Look, if she say no, wait 'til she go to bed and just open your window and come out to meet me. I'm leaving Saturday night."

"I can't—I—I can't do that."

"*I can't* means I *won't. Can't* never could do nothing. Oh, so what you saying is you don't want to be with me."

"Well yeah, I do, but—"

"Then what you worried about? You get ready and let's go!"

"Okay, but first you got to talk to her. See what she say."

●

Lula sat on the porch with a bowl of cornbread and pot liquor when a pregnant young woman ran into her yard. "Lady, can I sit on your porch to get away from him?" she said. Lula noticed a young man running towards her, so she opened the screen door and retrieved the rifle she used for hunting. The man was charging after the woman, but when he saw Lula raise the rifle to her shoulder, the man stopped running and started talking.

"That's my wife!" he said. "You and nobody else gonna keep me away from her. This ain't your business. You don't know what she did, so gon' back in your house and mind your business."

The young woman began to cry. "Please don't let him hurt me."

Lula said, "You're right. I don't know what she did. But let me tell you what I do know. I know she's pregnant. I know that this here is private property, and I know that you are trespassing. Oh yeah… I also know that this is a loaded rifle, and if you take one more step on my land, I'm going to put a bullet in your heart. I know that!"

With that the young man backed away. He went down the road shouting, "I don't need her anyway! I got me somebody. I got a mama *and* a grandma. I don't need her!"

Lula took off her apron and offered it to the woman who proceeded to wipe away her tears.

"You want to talk about what happened?" Lula said.

The woman started folding the apron into tiny pleats. "He came home from work early. I didn't feel good this morning, so I was still in bed. He complained because the house wasn't cleaned up. Then he told me to get up and fix him something to eat. I told him I didn't feel good. That made him mad. Said he was tired of me being sick. Said he was sorry he married me. Said I used to be cute, but now I looked like an elephant. I started to cry. I said he the cause of it. Then he grabbed me by the throat and pushed me against the wall. I raised my knee and kicked him in his soft spots. He screamed and doubled over, and I ran out of the house."

"Well…you did good. Now what?"

"I don't know. I ain't got nobody. No people. No big brother to make him behave right. I don't know what I'm gon' do. Ain't nobody gon' let me work 'cause I'm big. I don't know how I can live without him."

"Oh, you'll find a way. But you have to really want it. I'm sorry this happened to you, especially since you are pregnant. But this is the kind of thing that you can't go over or under or around. You will have to go directly through it. You are the only one who can stop it. Once you figure out that stopping it is what you want, the rest will be easy." Lula took the woman's hand. "When you feel like it is time for that baby to come let me know. I am right here every day. I'll help you deliver. You hear?"

"Yes, Ma'am."

After a while the woman left Lula's porch and walked in the direction from which she had come—back, Lula thought, to her home. Back to an abusive man.

So, Lula was still holding the rifle when she noticed another young man approaching. She pushed her skirt down between her legs and closed her knees. At first, she thought he might be selling something. Yes, another Bible salesman. Then she noticed that he was not carrying a satchel, so she assumed that he was either lost or he went to school with Pearl. She called the girl to the front porch.

"What's your name, boy?" Lula asked him.

"Name's Weldon Robert Hopwood, Ma'am." He wore glasses, a Sunday suit, and a big grin. He held his hat in both hands, and the look in his eyes was like a dog at the dinner table waiting for someone to drop something. "I came to ask your permission to marry Pearl. We want to move to Philadelphia."

Lula stood up and looked at the sky.

"Was there a full moon last night?"

"Ma'am?"

"*Or...*or maybe this is try Lula day!"

"Sorry, Ma'am. I don't understand."

"What you mean marry Pearl? You ain't even had time to court yet."

"That's because she said you would not let her court."

"Ain't nobody asked me a thing." She looked accusingly at her daughter.

He adjusted his tie and cleared his throat. Miss Lula, may I have permission to court Miss Pearl?"

Lula stood up. "Hell no! This girl is too young for courting. And she definitely too young to go traipsing off into no man's land with some crazy boy."

Pearl looked directly at Weldon and whispered, "Told ya." She turned to her mother. "Mama, I'm fifteen. Please. I'm old enough." She started to cry.

"Oh no, Ma'am. I ain't crazy," Weldon said.

"You must be crazy if you think you gon' take my daughter off and beat up on her when there ain't nobody to protect her."

"I wouldn't beat Pearl. I love her."

"Yeah. That's what they all say until they get you. This girl is going to college. I will not let her ruin her life by running off with some broke ass man. Now you get the hell out of my yard."

"I may be broke now, but they got plenty of good jobs in Philadelphia, and I'm going to get me one of 'em. With a fancy name like mine, I am sure to get hired somewhere."

"Uh huh. You do that. Then maybe we can talk."

Weldon could tell by the frosty sternness in Lula's face that she meant business, and he did not protest further. Instead, he stepped down from Lula's porch and walked away. He never even looked at Pearl.

Lula and Pearl went to bed that night without talking about Weldon. Pearl was still crying. Lula awoke the next morning before the rooster crowed. She had an eerie feeling that something was wrong. She felt a draft, and as she headed to the front of the house, she noticed the open window in her daughter's room. Pearl was gone.

Now Lula felt empty. Alone. She had been abandoned by her own mother and then by Lula B. She had been abandoned by Foots Walker, and now by his child. She decided that there must be something wrong with her to make people leave her that way, and she determined that it would never happen again. By now Susu and Sally were forever gone, and Lula felt a sensation she had never been able to imagine.

She felt the urge to work, to do something with her hands to replace the vacuum in her heart. She chopped some wood and started a fire in the big cauldron outside. She went to the well and drew buckets of water, sloshing it on her skirt and the ground as she walked. In a frenzy, she stripped Pearl's bed and threw the sheets into the boiling water. She used her homemade lye soap to scrub them. When she hung them up to dry, she realized that it was not enough. She was filled with fury. She grabbed her own sheets and threw them into the pot. She took down the curtains and washed them, too. Lula was fuming. Seething. Her breath was rapid and liquid. She scrubbed the floors, cabinets, walls and front porch. She poured the cleaning water into the yard and swept it down to eliminate the foot tracks and everything that reminded her of Foots and Pearl. All the while she was fussing and screaming—*I did the best I could. The best I knew how to do. Now, all gone—all gone. I made room for you in my house. I made room for you in my bed. I even found a place for you in my heart. I gave you all I had, and it still wasn't enough. You left me with that girl, and I loved her. Loved her! Now, she's gone, too.*

By the end of the day Lula was worn out. She felt drained, like her feelings had been ground and pressed through a sieve. She bathed in cold water, rubbing her skin vigorously. She was too old to pick up her former ways, and the horrible truth lay in the fact that one could love or one could hate, be hot or cold, be caring or pitiless, it did not matter. Pain follows distance *and* closeness.

She dried herself, stepped into a pair of bloomers and went to bed. From this point forward, Lula would regard life and the living with indifference.

Part Two

65

Lula B

Six

By the time Bee reached the store on Highway 42 she
was wet with sweat. It was a hot August day, and she had
walked the six miles as if she had a mission. When she
got there, she sat on the horse bar for a few minutes to
compose herself before entering the store. For a moment
she felt a new thing: fear. What if the sun set before she
got to Wilson? Where would she stay until tomorrow?
She had not brought a thing to eat and her stomach was
feeling a little faint. She knew, however, that she could
not go back to her mother's house. Not now. She felt
vulnerable and alone. But she was determined to make
it on her own, even if it meant starving to death, so Bee
wiped the sweat from her face and went into the store.

She did not see him at first, but she felt uncomfortable,
like she was on display. Bee pretended to shop—looking
at fabric, looking at candies—and finally, she looked up
to meet eyes with a very handsome man. Neither of them
said anything; they just stared at each other until the
moment became awkward. Bee was the first to move. She
wandered over to the counter and asked the man there
about her destination.

"Excuse me, Sir. How far is it to Wilson?"

He glared at her briefly. This little colored gal, pretty
as she may be, dared to look him in the face as she spoke.

He pointed towards the west.

"It's about twelve miles that way."

It had taken her all day to walk this far. She thought about the descending sun and her fear of the dark. She would have to sleep in the woods where all kinds of creatures would love a taste of her flesh.

"What time is it now, Sir?"

The man looked at the clock on the wall. "Can't you tell time, gal? It's twenty minutes to three."

Bee did not answer his question. There had never been a need to learn how to tell time. She nodded politely and excused herself. She went back outside to assess her situation. The man who had been staring at her came out almost immediately.

"You trying to get to Wilson?"

"Yes, Sir."

"You got people there?"

"No. No, Sir."

"Well, what's in Wilson?"

"I don't know, Sir. Guess I'll have to find that out."

They both laughed a little then. And Bee, fidgeting a bit, quickly added: "I'm gonna find me a job!"

It was a notion she had not entertained, but in that instant, it made sense to her.

"What's your name?"

"Lula B. Cooper, Sir." She shrugged her shoulders. "My mama's name is Lula, so folks call me Bee."

"I see. Kinda like Lula, Jr.?"

She laughed. "Why, yes Sir. Kinda like that."

"Well, Bee...you shouldn't be out here by yourself. It's dangerous for a pretty little thing like you. I'm going that way." He tilted his head towards his buckboard. "You want a ride?"

She thought for a minute as she eyed him cautiously. He didn't seem threatening. He was tall and considerably older than she was, and he appeared to be a gentleman. He was a strong and handsome man. Broad shoulders and long, stable legs. Her only alternative would be to find a tree in the woods to spend the night. By riding into town with him she could save all her money, she reasoned.

"What is your name?" Bee said.

"John Davies."

"Well, Mr. Davies, I'd love to take that ride."

He helped her onto the seat and untied the horse. During the trip to Wilson, they talked about little things: the weather, the price of dry goods. At last, he said to her, "If you don't have people in town, I suppose you will need a place to stay."

Bee had not thought about that. In fact, she had thought of nothing except getting away from her mother. "Yes, Sir," she said.

"I have a piece of land on the east side of town. It has a house on it that's in pretty good shape. It's empty right now, and it's yours if you want it. You don't have to pay rent or anything. Just keep it up so it will bring a good price if I ever decide to sell it." Suddenly his face brightened like the sun was inside it. "Matter of fact, that could be your job! I will keep you supplied with food and clothes, and you can just keep up my property. How does that sound?"

"That's fine," Bee said, and she looked away from him.

Sensing her resistance, he said, "You don't have to stay forever. Just until you get on your feet."

"Thank you," she said. "I can do that, Mr. Davies."

"Call me John."

"Okay. I can do that, John."

He moved her to the far east corner of Wilson, North Carolina, and, true to his word, he provided her every need. He brought her food and clothes every week as he traveled back and forth from the General Store. Once a month he would go to Greenville or Goldsboro, and he would always stop by to check on her. Most of the time he could find her working her garden, but on the rare occasion when she was not at home, he'd drive down to Contentnea Creek and find her fishing. They shared a love for fresh fish and he learned early that the creek was the only place she went without telling him.

He brought flowers and shrubs for the yard. Azalea bushes for the front and boxwoods for the back. The azaleas would be dormant for the winter, but with proper care they would have beautiful blooms in the spring. He helped her plant marigolds and October roses. A crepe myrtle and two dogwood trees.

There was a stray cat that roamed the property. The cat peed on one of the boxwoods and killed it. Bee was angry with the cat, and she used her broom to scare it away every day. But the cat continued to sleep on her back porch, and before long she had a litter of kittens. Now, Bee understood why her plant had died. Pregnant cat pee will kill just about anything. So, she started feeding the cat, and she named her Miss Kitty.

At first Miss Kitty would run away when Bee approached her, as if she were remembering the broom. But she always ate the food that Bee left on the porch. Miss Kitty made a spot for herself at the end of the yard, and she would feed her kittens there. One by one the little ones disappeared and before long there was only one kitten left. The two of them, Miss Kitty and her son, would eat whatever Bee put out for them. The cats were good company for her. They never tried to come into the house, but every morning when Bee opened her curtains, there they were waiting and meowing for their breakfast. The kitten had a snow-white breast and white feet all the way up to the joints of his legs. Bee named him *Socks* and the three of them—Miss Kitty, Socks, and Bee—eventually became a family.

One day when Bee opened the curtains there was a huge male cat sitting and waiting with the others. The three of them all looked alike, gray and black and white with rings around their tails. They were having a family moment, and, for a while, Bee felt a twinge of loneliness and isolation. The male cat left after he ate, but he returned every morning for breakfast. Early one Sunday morning the male cat arrived late. Miss Kitty and Socks had already started their meal. As he approached the bowl, Miss Kitty smacked him across his face with her right front paw, and then she stood with a hump in her back as if she were daring him to eat. Bee giggled at that. It was a moment of resolution. He could not stay out all night and then come home to a ready meal. Under those circumstances, Bee named the male cat *Alley.*

With the onset of winter John cut down a few trees and chopped them into firewood to keep her warm. Bee watched with enthusiasm as he worked. She stood at the kitchen window and found herself daydreaming about what it would be like to kiss him. Once in a while he would catch her staring at him. He smiled and waved and went right back to work. She, in turn, rewarded him with a hot meal before he left. And while he never made any demands on her, he lovingly gave her small gifts—candy, ribbons for her hair, a jar of whiskey. He gave her two dollars every week, a kind of allowance for incidentals, and she kept the money in a fruitcake tin. Because John provided her needs, there was never a reason to spend it.

●

John Davies had a wife and two children on the west side of town. His wife came from a good family, well-known and respected. And rich. But she lacked passion. She insisted on making love in absolute darkness, and once during a flash of lightning, he caught a glimpse of her face. She was staring at the ceiling as if she were praying for him to finish. She was completely detached from their conjugal moments. Often, she would grit her teeth in her sleep and mumble "Leave me alone" if he accidentally touched her in the night. He knew in his heart that she only did it because she thought she had to do it. He tried to explain that it was an important part of being married, and when he asked her about her lack of participation, she admitted that she just did not like it.

"I don't like the way your sweat drips down onto my face. And I do *not* like that slipperiness between my legs."

John was hot-blooded and virile. He could go three times a night if she would let him. He decided to compromise.

"I can't do anything about the sweat, but all I need is five minutes of your time three times a week."

"Two. Make it two and we have a bargain."

So that was the extent of his love life. An obligatory tumble scheduled precisely at nine o'clock at night on Tuesdays and Thursdays. She surrendered with these exact words: "Let's just get this over and done with." Whenever she delivered a heavy sigh, he knew his time had expired and he needed to finish quickly.

John was an important man in Wilson—big in business, big in community involvement. Because he married money, he had good, powerful friends. His best longtime friend was Jesse Landers. They had known each other since their school days. They each had joined the army and spent four years traveling the world. When they returned to Wilson, they started a business together importing dry goods and guns from Europe.

Snow Hill was the main trading artery that connected Wilson and other towns to New Bern. The cargo ships would come into port at New Bern and the merchandise would be transported by wagon to Snow Hill. In previous years it had been a primary source for slave trading. Now, its focus was on copper, cloth, rum, and guns and ammunition. Many merchants traveled there by boat, following Contentnea Creek until it emptied into the Neuse River. They collected their merchandise and took it back to their stores in Wilson, Goldsboro, Greenville and other neighboring towns. It required the men to be away from home for days, sometimes weeks at a time. It was often good for their marriages because when they returned home, their wives were glad to see them.

But it was different for John. His wife greeted him with indifference. She never seemed excited about anything— the embroidered handkerchief, the many bottles of perfume, or even the yards of silk he had ordered from

England especially for her. He expected some kind of reward for that.

He started to make his visits to Bee three, maybe four, times a week. He made up some kind of excuse to be there—plant a new tree or build a fence or lay a brick walkway that led to the house. Like Bee, John had fantasized a moment of intimacy, but neither knew the other had thought about it. They had been friends now for two years, and had it not been for the fact that they were so different in age and race, they might have been a perfect union. He would work in the yard or fix something in the house; she would have a meal ready for him when he finished. But the world was not yet ready for the likes of them as a couple. Well, at least Wilson wasn't.

It so happened that on one of these *work visits* as John was washing up and preparing to leave, Bee offered him a glass of whiskey.

"Celebrate with me," she said. "It's my birthday."

He was more than willing to do that; he was eager. He had wanted her badly from the day he saw her, but she was young, and his sense of honor disallowed him to force her into anything. "Thank you," he said with a smile.

She motioned for him to sit at a table, and she served him roast beef, fried cabbage and potatoes stewed with bacon and onion. He ate heartily. They laughed and talked, and eventually, John found himself confessing his fantasy.

"I have waited for a woman like you all my life," he said.

"And I belong to you," she said. "You don't even have to ask."

She was not a virgin. She believed that the white boys she had known behind the barn at the Cooper Plantation had taught her about how to please a man. For many months she had been so hot for John that she thought she would boil over, but because he never seemed interested, she had found other ways to put out the fire. He was good to her, and she certainly did not want to ruin that by being overly aggressive.

Now, the whiskey warmed them both. She leaned forward and parted her lips. In her eyes he saw a sign of welcome. She was tall and pretty with light skin and wavy hair. She had saddle hips that swayed from side to side, and just enough breasts to be interesting. He cupped her face and kissed her. "I could eat you up," he said.

"That's funny. I was just thinking that I could lick you all over."

"Where would you begin?"

"Do you really want to know?"

"Yes!"

There was no blush in her. She was now a grown woman, and her behavior towards him was that of a grown, experienced woman.

"I would start with your mouth, your lips."

"And then?"

"Then I would trail my tongue across your face to your ears, your neck. I would be very gentle, but I would nibble at your shoulders, your chest, your belly." She moved her hand over his body as she spoke. "I would take a detour at your hips and lick your thigh on the outside. Then I would cross your knee and lick my way up your inner thigh to your testicles. I would massage that long vein in your shaft with my tongue until it throbs and begs me to take you into my mouth."

"Oooooh, my, my, my!"

He lifted her and carried her to bed. Bee followed the exact route she had laid out for him. He came and she swallowed. He pledged himself to her forever. They made love for the rest of the evening. Her response was full of genuine passion. She gave herself to him fully, willingly, without trickery, and Bee became the secret that was not really a secret. It never occurred to either of them that someone was watching.

Seven

IN THE SPRING OF **1896** JOHN PURCHASED A BROUGHAM from Anderson and Woodward in Black Creek. He drove into Bee's yard as she was cleaning a chicken for dinner. By now Miss Kitty and a few other generations of cats had disappeared, but they were continually replaced by others. At this time Bee's husband and wife cat couple were Chloe and Sebastian. They ran to hide under the porch as John arrived.

The carriage was made of dark mahogany and cherrywood trim. It came equipped with a chamber pot and face towels. The cab had two seats of tufted velvet that faced each other. Of course, they were red! John's horse led the rig.

"Look at you, Mr. Fancy!" Bee said. "What happened to your buckboard?"

"I still have it. I bought this for you."

"For me?"

"I thought you might be getting tired of riding that old mule."

Bee laughed. "That old mule 'bout tired of me riding him."

"I was thinking about running down to New Bern just to watch the ships come in. Want to take a ride?"

"You think that's safe?"

"Well sure. Nobody's going to bother *me*. I'm John Davies."

"All right!" she said. "Let me just clean up a bit."

"Um, Bee...how about you wear that hat I brought you last week. The one with the veil? And put your gloves on."

It was a cool, crisp morning. Bee felt like a princess as she peered out of the small window and noticed the singing birds, the blooming trees, and the lacy rows of newly sprouted tobacco and vegetables, the animals and the many farm workers doing their daily tasks. John sat erect and proud as he drove their little vehicle along the road, an occasional wave or tipping of the hat to fellow travelers. They drove until the sun set and, figuring they were about halfway to their destination, they stopped, fed and watered the horse and spent the night in the carriage.

Bee awoke to the smell of bacon and coffee. The door to the carriage was open. "Morning," she said, and she put her foot on the running board in an effort to join John by the fire.

"No!" he said. "Stay where you are."

He looked around nervously and then, realizing that he might have hurt her feelings, he said. "I am at your service today, my lady. This is your vacation."

After breakfast John put out the fire and they resumed their trip to New Bern. They arrived about supper time. There was a familiar place where John generally stayed when he was there on business. The rooms were comfortable, and the food was decent. He walked in and went straight to the desk with Bee trailing him at a short distance. The clerk recognized him immediately.

"Evening, Mr. Davies. How can I help you today?"

"I need a room...for about two days, I reckon."

"Why, yes Sir. Right away, Sir. I see you got the missus with you this time."

John looked at Bee. He had not thought of how he could explain her presence. "Yes, but she's feeling poorly. The trip wore her out."

"Oh, I understand that. Long ride from Wilson."

"Listen," John said. "I'm going to take her to our room, and I'll come back and get her some supper after we get settled. Will that be all right?"

"Absolutely, Sir. Here is your key. It's the second room on the right at the top of the stairs. Just sign here."

John signed the registry as 'Mr. and Mrs. John Davies,' and he escorted his *wife* to their room. They spent the entire next day walking along the shore gazing at the ships, watching them load and unload. They shopped the stores near the shipyard, and he bought her a bar of sweet soap and a crystal bracelet. He fastened the bracelet over her glove and made sure her veil was intact before they returned to their room.

Like the night before, John went downstairs to get supper for them. As he was about to ascend the stairs, he heard a voice call his name.

"John! John Davies! Is that you?"

He turned to face Stuart Wallace, one of the deacons in his wife's church.

"Yes, it's me." He stacked one plate on top of the other to extend his hand. "How do you do?"

"I'm good. Good." Stuart eyed the two plates. "Little hungry tonight, John?"

They both laughed. "Yes. What are you doing in New Bern?"

"Oh, we have a revival this week. Folks coming from all over the state. You should come. You know, you really ought to come to church more often, John. And bring Ellen. Haven't seen her in a while, either. She doing all right?"

"Yes, she's fine."

"Well, tell her I said hello. Good to see you, John."

"I'll do that."

The men parted and John exhaled a sigh of relief. That was close. Too close. It was time to go, so he and Bee left New Bern at about midnight when everyone else was asleep.

They drove through the night and much of the next

day. When they arrived at Bee's place, John unhitched his horse and mounted it quickly.

"You must be tired," Bee said. "Don't you want to spend the night?"

"No. I need to get back to the house. I'll be back in a couple of days."

A little down-hearted, Bee headed towards her back porch. There she saw Chloe and Sebastian engaged in what she thought was an argument. There was a funny sound to Chloe's meow, almost like a song. Sebastian's voice, deep and groaning, sang in harmony with her.

They stood face to face and Bee noticed that Chloe's tail was up and there was no hump in her back. They did not move, even as Bee stomped her foot and tried to shoo them away. "Oh!" she said. "I get it!" She went into the house and gave them privacy.

●

When John arrived home, he was met at the door by his wife. She wore a smile and a lacy white gown. She had a drink in her hand, which she offered to him. He thanked her and went straight to their room. The look on her face let him know that this was one of those rare occasions when she wanted to be intimate. He got in bed and turned his back to her.

"John…" she said. "You've been gone a long time. Aren't you going to bother me tonight?"

"No thanks. I'm tired. I just want to sleep."

"John!"

It was a moment of sheer pleasure. All these years of begging her; now she was begging him. He could not resist the smile that crept over his face as she beat him on his back. He wouldn't touch her now even if he were aroused. Give her a taste of what it's like to be rejected. Let her see how it feels.

"John. I am your wife!"

He said nothing. He just lay there and thought of Bee, his real wife, until he went to sleep.

•

Ellen Westcott Davies was a proud woman. She was raised in a wealthy family, made so by buying and selling slaves and land. Her mother taught her that there was nothing in the world too good for her. She also taught her about the power she held between her legs. "A woman can get whatever she wants by giving or withholding," her mother once said.

Ellen had married John Davies because of his military experience and because she could see the potential in him. She gave him two children—two fine boys, and she saw that as the extent of her obligations as his wife. She enjoyed being Mrs. Davies, but only as far as the prestige it provided for her. The afternoon teas and bridge games with her close friends gave her much more pleasure. She was a leader in her society, and she orchestrated many charity functions. All this she did on purpose to maintain the high opinion the general public held of her. But she wanted more from her husband—more power and more recognition.

So, when the City Council members came to speak with John about supporting him in a run for governor, she was very excited. John was away on business, she told them, but she would speak with him as soon as he returned. Her method was to swallow her pride and let him have his way with her. That way he would be open when she made the suggestion.

But it did not work that way. He was too tired to make love. She would have to develop another plan. Perhaps she would even be straightforward and let him know that she deserved to be First Lady of North Carolina. The way he treated her last night, however, made her think that perhaps she was losing her grip. She had always been able to get her way by offering him sex. And while she had heard stories about how he spent his time away from her, there was never a threat that he would leave her. He always pestered her when he came home. This time he had turned her down, and that caused her to wonder why.

She sent a message to Mr. Cousins, a man with a reputation for being very thorough and very, very discreet. In the morning John went to the kitchen. Without speaking Ellen poured coffee and set it in front of him.

"What are your plans today?" she said finally.

In almost twenty years of marriage, she had never asked him about his business or how his day would go. Her question made him suspicious of her inquiry.

"I have some errands to run. Won't take long. Why?"

"I need you to be here at noon. Some of the members of City Council are coming by. They want to talk with you."

"About what?"

"I am not sure. Just be here to speak with them." Realizing that she may have sounded too abrupt, too demanding, she added, "Please."

So, John put forth the effort to be at home on time to entertain the gentlemen from Wilson City Council. There were six men in his house when he arrived. They sat in the parlor smoking cigars. They exchanged pleasantries while Ellen busied herself pouring tea and delivering cookies and napkins. The men seemed to be hesitant to get into the real purpose of their visit in front of her, so John made a motion with his head, and she left the room.

"Now John," one of the men began. "We have put a lot of thought into this. It's about time North Carolina got a Governor from Wilson. We want you to run."

"Me? I don't know the first thing about running the State of North Carolina."

"Well, we will teach you. First thing though, we want you to run for City Council so you can get some experience in government."

He eyed the men curiously. "Why me? Why not one of you?"

"First of all, you are a successful businessman with a good, clean record of dealing with people. Your reputation is excellent. Then there's Ellen. She has all the qualities of the First Lady. She feeds the hungry, conducts the church bazaar, and she knows all the right people. She is a born leader. She even tells us men what to do."

John chuckled a little. "I guess I am interested. Tell me more."

"City elections are in about ten months. We will get your name on the ballot. You are guaranteed to win. The state elections are in three years. We will train you and, by that time, you will know exactly what to expect and how to win."

"Sounds good," John said, and for the first time in years he was excited about something other than Lula B.

●

About a month after their trip Bee was sitting on the porch when Chloe rubbed herself against Bee's leg. She said, "What's the matter? You pregnant? Guess what? Me too."

She had not seen John in almost a week, but she trusted him, and she believed he would be happy about the baby. They had been together for ten years, so this was very exciting news. She decided to make a game of telling him, a kind of play that was peculiar to adults in love, especially them. She made notes and placed them in little envelopes with numbers on them, and she situated them on items in the house. Nine altogether in a kind of connect-the-dot fashion.

So, when John came that Saturday she asked him, "Do you see anything different about me?"

She had parted her hair down the middle and braided each side. "You did something different with your hair," he said.

"Not that, silly. Do you see anything else?"

He was embarrassed, and he was not good at playing games. "No."

"All right. I'll give you a hint. There are nine envelopes in this house, and you have to find each one in order. Even if you find another one, don't read it out of order. Okay?'

He decided to humor her. "Okay."

The first one was on the back door. It read "Guess." He found number two on the table.

"What?" He could not find number three until she stood by her apron hanging on the wall.

"You." Number four was on the coffee pot. "Are." Number five was on the front door, which they never used. "Going." He found number six on the rag rug she had made. "To." Seven was on the bedroom door. "Be." Number eight was taped to the cedar chest at the foot of their bed. "Somebody's." And on the bed is where he found the last one. "Daddy."

John's mouth dropped open, and his eyes lit up like stars. "You are going to have a baby? A baby?!" He loosened her hair and made love to her right then in the middle of the day.

He always wanted more children. He did think, however, about the danger involved if anyone ever found out about them. The Klan could burn a cross on her yard or hurt their child. His wife could have her evicted from the property. All kinds of things ran through his mind, not the least of which was the notion of him running for Governor.

Still, when their first child was born, John was right there. Bee's plan had worked; their son was beautiful. They named him Frederick, and as soon as he was old enough to walk, they made another child, Margaret, whom they called Maggie. The last one, a girl they named Easter, was born in 1901.

Bee was a good mother and a good woman. She never complained about anything. Often, he could find her with Easter strapped to her back as she hacked cabbage or dug potatoes or killed a chicken. She sang as she cleaned snot or emptied the slop jar. Hummed when she washed clothes on a scrub board. Plowed and planted her garden. And with each passing day, John loved her more and more.

Eight

JOHN WAS A NATURAL POLITICIAN. HE LOVED WILSON AND HE was always looking for ways to improve it. He lived near the country store on Highway 58, but he was as familiar with the needs of city folks as anyone could be. He visited the elderly and hired colored men to cut their grass and paint their houses. He determined to line West Nash Street with beautiful trees, which he had purchased with his own money. He delivered the trees two at a time using his buckboard, and he placed them in the spots where they should go. Then he went to see Stuart Wallace.

"Howdy, Stuart," he said as he extended his hand. "What you know good?"

"John," Stuart said. His face was stern. He did not shake, so John withdrew his hand.

"Look, ah...I bought some trees to plant, and I was wondering if you could get some of the fellows from the church to put them in the ground for me."

"Maybe." The deacon stared at John's face, but he was not friendly.

"Well, tell them that I already put them where they should go. All they need to do is dig a hole for each of them. Tell them to use that fertile, black dirt."

"Like you, John?"

"Beg pardon?"

"I hear tell you been planting your tree in some fertile, black dirt, too."

John, embarrassed, pretended not to understand.

"What are you talking about? I haven't planted a tree in many years. My yard is very well appointed."

"I'm not talking about a damn yard, and you know it. I'm talking about that colored woman you got, and all them coffee-colored babies."

"Now, Stu, that's none of your business. Just leave it alone."

"Oh, it's my business all right. I've known your wife's family all my life. They are good friends and good *people*! Your secret is out, and it affects us all."

John turned to walk away. "Get the trees planted, all right?"

"You better stop what you doing, John. Can't no good come of it."

John was stunned by this revelation. He was unaware that everyone knew about Bee. He would have to be more careful, but he knew he could not quit her. She was the love of his life.

He was not the first white man to be in love with a colored woman, and he would not be the last. He was addicted to her, the smell of her, the heat of her body, and the absolute willingness to let him play with her. She gave herself to him without regard to time. A light burned on her front porch as a sign of uninterrupted invitation. He knew in his heart that she wanted him, was true to him; her participation was genuine. And while he was almost old enough to be her father, he had never experienced such passion and excitement with anyone. A fried pork chop and a cool glass of white lightning always served as a celebration when their encounters were over. He could count on her, and John Davies would not, *could not,* abandon Lula B. Cooper. Even when the children came, she was devoted and attentive to him. The babies were always clean and fed, and Bee made sure they were out of his way when he wanted to be with her.

John loved teaching things to his children with Bee—how to read and color, how to ride a bike. And the boy...he taught Fred how to shoot. He bought a shotgun especially for Fred so the child could shoot rabbits and protect their home.

On one of these visits, he brought Bee an official piece of paper. "Keep this in a safe place," he told her. "It is the deed to this house and it's in your name. If anything should happen to me, I fixed it so that this will always be your home. If anything ever does happen to me, I want you to make sure Easter gets this land when you are gone."

Easter was the favorite of all his children with both Bee and Ellen. She was a feisty little thing, full of energy and quick-tempered. John called her *Short Fuse*. But she was also smart and business-minded. John noticed this when he gave her a nickel to purchase a small toy, a spinning top. Fred wanted the toy and he and Easter fought over it. Finally, she sold the top to Fred for seven cents. She had made a profit, and John wanted to encourage that part of her.

As he left Bee's house that day, he did not notice Mr. Cousins posted by a tree, but he felt uneasy. He sensed that Stuart Wallace was dangerous to him and to Bee and their children. So, the next day John returned with a pick and shovel and a month's worth of food and supplies. There was a five-gallon drum of water and plenty of canned goods. He went to work immediately digging out a space under the house. He worked feverishly, with urgency so as to complete the job on that day.

"What are you doing, John?" Bee wanted to know.

"I'll tell you later. Tell Fred to come here."

By nightfall the job was done. John and Fred, father and son, worked side by side building the safe place. When they sat down to table, John told the family about his plan.

"Listen, Bee. Things are changing and money is tight for a while."

"Don't worry about that. I have more than $1600 saved." She smiled proudly. "I never spent a dime of my allowance in all these years."

"Good. Woodrow Wilson has got us into a World War. He also re-established the income tax. Tariffs were bad enough, but Jesse and I could always figure out a way to sneak something into the country without paying them. Now, with income tax...well, it's going to cut into our profits. Taxes can't be played with. Anybody try to avoid paying *them* is going to jail."

"You can have the money I saved up if you need it."

"No. You keep that for you and the children. There are some strange things going on in Wilson right now. I don't mean to frighten you, but I want you to know what to do if anything ever happens."

"You keep talking about something happening, John. And that *does* scare me."

"Don't be scared. Just be ready. I dug out a spot for you and the children to go if anybody should come here to hurt you. There is plenty of food down there. And water. I left an oil lamp and there is a little peephole so you can get air and see who is out there."

"John...?"

"Bee! Promise me you will take care of my children."

She was confused and frightened, but she knew him well. Pressing him for an answer would not help the situation.

"I promise," she said.

●

John was never elected Governor. He had lost the bid to Charles Brantley Aycock in 1900, and after a brief attempt to run in 1904, he dropped out of the race. Ellen wanted him to try again in 1908, but the lust for power and recognition could not compete with his desire for Bee. He did not want to be Governor, and, in truth, Ellen had already found out about Lula B.

John walked into his house one day just as Mr. Cousins was leaving. They exchanged greetings, and though he was curious as to the contents of the large envelope Cousins carried, he did not ask about it. He was equally unaware of the tempest he was about to encounter.

"Where have you been, John?"

"Since when do you care?"

"Since I found out about your little trollop across town."

He raised his brows, but he said nothing.

"Oh, don't look so surprised. And don't try to deny it, either. I have had you followed for years!"

"Why?"

"Because I knew you were doing *something.* I had no idea that it was a *nigger* bitch!"

"Woman, you watch your mouth. Don't talk about Lula B. that way."

"Oh. Lula B. is it? You can stand there and defend her to me? How dare you!? The whole town knows. You did it on purpose. You did it to humiliate me!" She paced the floor in a strut that John recognized as her way of exhibiting power in her rightness.

He put his hat on the table. "I wasn't trying to humiliate you."

"What were you trying to do? Were you trying to replace me? Did you think you could be sworn in as Governor with a black bitch by your side. What exactly were you trying to do, John?"

"I was trying to be happy!" He didn't mean to raise his voice, but he needed her to hear him beyond her anger. "I love her."

That seemed to stop her in her tracks. She welled up, but her pride would not let her cry in front of him. With a swift movement of her hand, she wiped away the tear that threatened to fall, and she raised her chin. "What about me?"

He swallowed hard. "God help me. I love you, too."

"And our sons? Did you ever think about them, John?"

"You know I love those boys—"

"You don't even *know* them!"

John hung his head, and for a minute it looked like he was going to cry. Ellen resisted the urge to hold him. He was still her husband after all, and she could see the pain in him. She wanted to comfort him, but she was filled with anger, vitriol, *rage.* She wanted to throw something. She wanted to break his face. But she could not let him know the devastation she suffered in knowing that he would choose *that woman* over her.

"No wonder you couldn't get elected. Everybody knows your dirt! You have to be punished for what you did, John. I spoke with my lawyer this morning. I am not going to file for divorce. Oh no! That would make it too easy for you to spend time with that *nigger* woman and her little *nigger* children. By staying with you I will get the sympathy of the entire community. I will be seen as the dutiful and forgiving wife. That's right. Your little indiscretion will not affect me and my reputation at all. It can only make me look like a strong woman who stands by her man in his time of weakness. But I have arranged it so that you get nothing. *Nothing,* John. You can stay here, but don't ever try to come to my bed again." She sat briefly and put her hands to her face. Just as quickly, she rose again. "Thirty-six years. We've been together for thirty-six *fucking* years!" Her use of that word shocked them both and she briefly covered her mouth with her hand. "See what you've done? I can't believe you would do this to me. To *me!*"

With that she stormed out, leaving John alone with his thoughts.

●

Then, in 1911, something happened that frightened John to the point that he could barely remain functional. He went to see Bee immediately and he called the entire family together.

"We need to do a practice run to your safe place," he told them. "Things are going on right now and the whole town is restless, white and colored alike."

Bee placed her hand on her chest. "John, what is it?"

"A colored man escaped jail last week. In the process he shot two white men. One of them was Deputy Mumford and the other one was Chief Glover. Mumford died. There is a statewide manhunt for this guy, Lewis West. When they find him, they are going to give him the chair if it gets that far. I'm worried, Bee. I'm worried and scared for you and the children."

"Why? What's that got to do with us?"

"In case you haven't noticed, Fred is a colored boy. The fellows are all sitting around and drinking and talking shit about what all they are going to do when they catch this guy. These people are crazy when they get liquored up. They don't care about description; all they see is a colored man. They can turn into a lynch mob quicker than you can blink an eye. Now, I want you all to follow me quietly and quickly. Show me that you know how to take advantage of the place I provided for you."

Fear gripped them, but they obeyed John. He blew out the candles and they all moved swiftly. In a minute they were in the shelter. John lit another candle and locked the trap door.

They were safe. The rehearsal was satisfactory. John could return to his home on the west side of town where he could keep an eye and ear close to the white community.

Lewis West was found hiding in a swamp in Greene County. The murder happened on February 3, 1911, and punishment was swift and severe. West was executed on May 5, of that same year.

But no one ever burned a cross on Bee's yard. No one threatened to harm her children.

John had some power left in that regard, and she was protected by him. By now, Wilson had two General Stores, one on Highway 58 near John's home, and the other one on 264 near hers. They were both owned by whites who were friends and business associates of John's. Bee held her head high on the rare occasion that she shopped at the one nearest her for fabric or ground coffee. She was acutely aware of the discerning looks she received during her visits to town, but her mission was always quick and direct, and then she would go back home to her haven.

No. It was John, instead, who encountered direct accusations. He was counseled by the preacher at Ellen's church. He was scorned by her relatives. He lost business, and as a result, he lost the friendship of Jesse Landers.

"We don't have many friends left in this town, John," Jesse said.

"Oh, they will come around. Some of them are simply jealous that I can get away with it that's all."

"No. That's not all. Have you looked at the books lately? No, of course you haven't. You've been too busy with that colored woman."

"Oh, my Lord. You, too, Jesse? Why can't you all just leave it alone? I keep telling you to mind your own business."

"It *is* my business, John. I know you better than anyone I reckon. At first, I thought you were just having some fun. Dipping your spoon into a little brown sugar. Hell, I have done that myself. But you fucked around and lost your *goddamn* mind!"

"I did not lose my mind! I didn't even have one until I met her."

"My boy is getting ready to go to college and I can't even pay for it. Shit. It's all I can do lately to keep food on the table."

"Things will get better in a while. I'm smart. I know how to build and rebuild a business. Can't nobody beat me in that regard." He had the nerve to be just a little bit arrogant about it. "This is only a temporary setback. I can rebuild this business."

"I don't think that's going to work, John. The women are the biggest shoppers and they all feel sorry for Ellen."

"I think I can rebuild Ellen's trust, too. She's upset right now, but she knows I will never leave her. She will get over it. I promise I can make her trust me again."

"Maybe you can. But I have decided to take a job over

in Rocky Mount."

"You going to leave me just like that? We've been friends our whole lives!"

"Friendship is one thing. Eating is another. Good luck, John."

Both Ellen and Stuart had warned him that the whole town knew about Bee, and now Jesse confirmed it. And just like that, it was over. John was left to fend for himself in his business and in his double life. The division of his time between Bee and her family and Ellen and hers weakened him and made him look older than his years. His sons with Ellen were grown, and they had eliminated him from their lives. They would not help him with his work, and they did not call on him for help with theirs.

What he did not know was that his friends and neighbors had been watching him. They kept up with his schedule, his travels to and from Bee's house. And they shared their observations with each other. Because he did not know this, he anticipated a loyalty that had become nonexistent. So it surprised him when he met with resistance from a group of his hunting buddies. Little did he know that it would be the last conversation he would have with them. It was August 17, 1915.

Nine

ON THE EAST SIDE OF **W**ILSON, **B**EE'S LAMENTATIONS WERE
loud and strong. She had read about John's death in the
newspaper. Neighbors gathered to comfort her. People
she did not even know came to offer condolences. Women
brought baskets of cooked meats and cakes. The men
prayed as they took big gulps of white lightning. It was
as close as she could get to a real funeral for John. Her
children, Fred, Maggie and Easter were near to hold her
hand and soothe her forehead with a cool cloth. Their
father had been murdered. Each of them would be
affected by this killing. The scandal. The shame of it all.
With John's death came the absence of protection. Yes.
The entire family was in danger and Bee needed time to
get away and decide what her next move should be.

She made the mistake of thinking she could find
comfort and encouraging words through her mother. She
had been gone for more than thirty years, and she was
not even sure her mother was still alive. But Susan had
taught her that blood was thicker than water, and she
was certain that her mother would be willing to forgive
and forget their troubles.

She wore widow's weeds and a black veil as she
drove her carriage into the yard. Lula was standing on
the porch, curious, surely, as to whom her visitor might

"

be. She rarely had company. In fact, the last person to even approach her doorstep was the U. S. Census taker of 1910. At that time, she had reported having only one child, Pearl. But while Pearl had run away in the middle of the night to marry, Lula hoped that *she* was the approaching visitor. She squinted her eyes and saluted her brows to guard against the early morning sun. Her back was bent, her face inquisitive, but when she recognized the daughter she had not seen in more than three decades, she straightened herself, walked into her house and slammed the screen door.

Lula and Bee had been enemies since the day that Bee decided that black was not good enough for her. That was the day that Bee had met John Davies. Now, with him gone, Bee dismounted the carriage and went into her mother's house.

"Hey, Ma."

Lula sat in her rocking chair looking out the window. She did not turn her head to greet her wayward daughter and, except to fill her bottom lip with Tube Rose, she did not open her mouth, either. Bee removed her pin and took off her hat and veil.

"It's good to see you."

"Look like you found somebody to take care of you. That true?"

"Yes, Ma'am."

"Then what you doing here, girl? Oh...oh, I know. That man done got tired of you, so you think you can just come back here, right?"

"He's dead, Ma."

"What?! How'd that happen?"

"The paper said somebody beat him to death."

"Uhm...Am I supposed to feel some kind of way about that?"

"I loved him, Mama."

"Love. Humph."

Then there was a long pause, long enough to soften Lula's heart a bit.

"Them your young'uns out there?"

"Yes, Ma'am."

"Well. I guess I always wondered if I had grandchil'ren. Bring 'em on in here. I got some lemonade in the ice box."

"Mama…I need your help. I don't know what to do." Bee started to cry.

"I said I got lemonade. Ain't got no help. This here is your bed, not mine. You made it; now you have to lie in it. You can wallow in corn husks, or you can fill it with chicken feathers. Up to you."

There was nothing else to say. The hatred had been allowed to fester too long. So, Lula B. took her family home. She did not introduce them to their grandmother.

●

Now, in the twilight of the day, Lula sat on her front porch. As was her habit, she watched the sun set. She knew at least that her first daughter was all right. Bee could find her way through this. Lula had raised her to be tough. It was a sad thing, having her man leave her like that, but that's what men do best. Whether they die or just walk out, it's all the same. Leaving is what they do best. She thought about Pearl. Did her man leave her, too? Was she even still alive? Did she have children and, if so, how many? Lula looked at her hands. Hardworking and old, but still capable. The rest of her was falling apart. Her legs hurt all the time. She could no longer work in the fields. At seventy-four years old she didn't have a single friend. She thought about Susan and wondered how long she would have been dead in that cabin if Lula had not gone to see her. She did not want that to happen to her—to die alone and rot away, offending all the animals in the forest with her stink, and attracting buzzards to fly over her house. And then she thought about Foots Walker. How could she have gotten that wrong? He was tall and handsome. She remembered how much he loved her cooking. The way they danced and played together, the sounds of nature providing the music for them. The way he swam in the pond. She thought of the rain and how close she felt to him. The comfort and joy he brought to her when he threw his leg over hers and held her while they slept. It was as if he was claiming her as his very own. She loved that feeling. And oh! How he could fuck. He was the best at that. She felt that happiness all over again. For a minute she stopped thinking to listen. A twitter of birds in the bushes. A cicada announcing the coming of night. A symphony of sounds that wrapped around her like a warm blanket. Then she heard a splash in the pond.

"Foots is back," she said. "Foots is back!"

She stood and walked toward the water. It was dark, but she was not afraid. "I'm coming baby," she said. "Wait for me. I'm coming..."

Step by slow step she walked into the water. Steady. Deliberate. "I'm coming baby."

She continued to walk deeper and deeper into the cool, still water.

"Wait for me. I'm coming Foots!"

And at last, the pond swallowed her whole.

Ten

ALONE BEE WOULD FINISH RAISING HER CHILDREN, WHICH wasn't much. Fred was almost nineteen, Maggie was seventeen. Easter was only sixteen and Bee had great plans for her.

Except that she was short, Easter was the spitting image of her father. Bee had no qualms about letting people know that Easter was her favorite. Every time she looked at her baby girl, she saw John. Easter's laughter, her walk—a strut, really—all reminded Bee of the man she had loved so hard. And she discovered early that Easter was gifted with her father's business sense. The child made rag dolls and sold them at the County Fair. She baked cakes and pies and sold them at the Church Association. She took in washing and sewing, and she was willing to do almost anything to make a quarter. Almost anything.

"This little girl is different from the rest," John had once said about Easter. "She is going to be somebody."

With that in mind, then, Bee chose to focus all her maternal attention on Easter. She would make sure the child was well dressed and well educated. Perhaps she could go to college and travel the world.

Bee, herself, was very well set. The house was hers forever. John had seen to that when he put the deed in her name. With peach and apple trees growing on her property, she had plenty of preserves in the shed, not to mention the canned goods in her safe place. A dozen chickens roamed the yard; bushels of potatoes cooled under the house, and slaughtered meat hung in the smokehouse. On occasion, she would travel to Contentnea Creek and catch a catfish for supper. Except for missing John, especially in the darkness of the night, she had no real problems.

Bee was a crafty woman, good with her hands. She could build things, like tables and chairs. She could make quilts and plow her garden. She could chop wood as well as any man, and she kept herself busy with work, hard work, to keep her mind occupied. She resolved to keep herself true to his memory. Determined to make current the fashion that had died ten years ago, she wore her skirts long. They dragged across the laces of her shoes.

Of course there were suitors. Men flocked to her door, often under the pretense of looking for work. The local mentality mandated that a single woman with children needed to be manned. She needed discipline and control. Moral support. Comfort in a way that only a man could provide. They came in droves, sometimes two or three a day, as if they all had a plan or a bet to see which of them could get to her first. But she turned them all away and focused instead on keeping her family safe.

She found humor in the introductory lines they used: *I can help you with them chil'ren...I need a woman like you...If you wait too long you gonna dry up.* Perhaps her favorite line to repeat was: *Better send for me early. I'm a busy man. I gets drunk, ya know.*

But then there was one that she simply called Mr. Battle. He worked at the General Store and he had to pass her house as he went to and from work. When she was working in the yard, he would stop just to say, "Morning, Miz Cooper," or "Evening, Ma'am," depending on the time of day. Their conversations were kept light and undirected, but as time went by, Bee took harbor in his short visits. It was a simple friendship filled with simple cordialities and simple gestures. Once in a while he would bend over and pluck a weed from her flower bed, but aside from this he never tried to suggest that she was lacking anything because she was a single woman with children. Bee liked that. He was important only because he was a man. Every woman needs a little male attention. But he was a gentleman, and he never crossed the line of friendship. Never took the liberty to call her by her first name, and he did not try to impose his special gifts on her.

She also found humor in watching the cats play. They brought her joy. Ever since Miss Kitty and Alley there had not been fewer than a dozen cats in her yard. She could sit on her porch for hours watching their habits. They would eat and then clean their paws and faces. Then the mother would lie down, and all the kittens would scramble to her breasts to nurse. After that they would wrestle with each other, bite ears and tails, and then take a long nap. One of the kittens had a very long tail, and she seemed surprised that it belonged to her. She'd crouch in a hunting position and stare at the tail. Then, when it moved, she'd attempt to pounce on it, but the tail escaped every time. Bee laughed until she cried.

As she wiped her tears with her apron, she thought of John. Every time. She missed him terribly. She knew that his love for her was real and everlasting. No man would ever be able to take his place, and Mr. Battle was the only man in town who seemed to know and respect that.

●

Easter bore the protective personality of her father. She loved being outside and when she was not working with her hands, she worked with her mind, planning, scheming and preparing for her future. She was very observant of other people, but she particularly enjoyed watching nature's critters. Birds were her favorite. She once saw a ladder-backed woodpecker that she tried, unsuccessfully, to catch with a fishing net. She paid close attention to the formation of birds as they flew past her house. She believed that birds showed special signs about the weather, about business, about relationships. She especially loved the musical honking of Canada Geese when they flew south for the winter or north for the summer. Twice a year the geese migrated, and Easter witnessed their travels each time. The lead bird knew the way and all the others followed in an arrow-like fashion. She likened the lead bird to herself because, while Fred and Maggie were both older than she, she was the one who knew how to get things done.

While she was washing dishes one day, Easter looked outdoors and saw a blue jay sitting quietly on her nest. One of the cats was trying to climb the tree. The cat was young and inexperienced, so Easter went outside to warn him about the nasty temperament of the bird. All of a sudden, the blue jay swooped down and pecked the cat rapidly on its head several times, and then she returned to her nest. She sat peering at the cat as it spun around in circles trying to figure out what had happened. When the cat got its bearings, it attempted to climb the tree again, and the bird repeated her attack. This went on for a few more minutes before the cat finally realized that maybe a lunch of blue jay was not worth the effort. It slithered off to hide under the azalea bush and Easter taunted the cat. "Be careful what you ask for. It ain't always what you want."

When she returned to the house, her family was in chaos. A blackbird had come through the open door and could not find its way out. Maggie was hiding under her bed. Bee was screaming at Fred to catch the bird, but he ran past Easter so fast he almost knocked her down.

"A black bird in the house means bad luck," Bee said.

The bird perched on the chandelier, its feathers ruffled, its eyes wide open.

Easter picked up her dish towel and slowly walked towards the trembling bird. She spoke softly. "It's okay, little birdie. Easter's gonna get you home."

She swiftly gathered the bird in the towel and walked back to the door to set it free.

Bee and Easter were a team. For the next few months, they worked together in the cotton fields. They cooked together every day, and they shared chores around the house. They hauled wood and coal and water, and they laughed at just about everything.

In fact, there were only two things about which Bee and Easter disagreed. The first was that Easter had a powerful temper, which is why her father nicknamed her Short Fuse. Just about anything could set her off. When she was a child, she had a disagreement with Maggie about the way Maggie had styled Easter's hair. She picked up a glass and threw it. Maggie ducked and the glass shattered against the door. Once when they were at the County Fair, a woman mentioned that she did not like the rug Easter tried to sell her. Easter punched the woman in the face and broke her nose. Bee had to pay the medical bills.

Shortly after her father died, Easter was raking leaves in the yard. She went into the house and filled a molasses jar with chunks of ice and some water. She liked to let it sit for a while until the outside of the jar had little beads of cold water. By the time she worked up a sweat, she went inside to get her drink only to find that Fred had drunk the water and left the pitiful little remains of ice in the jar. Easter was livid.

"Did you drink my water?"

"Oh, that was yours? I didn't see a name on it."

"You knew it wasn't yours!"

"What you getting so mad about? It's just water. Get you some more."

With that Easter opened the cabinet drawer and pulled out the butcher knife. "I'll kill you!" she said. She chased her brother down the dirt road until she was exhausted.

And he, afraid to sleep in the same house with her, packed his bag and left home.

Maggie went with him.

But aside from that and more importantly, Easter had inherited her grandmother's love for tall, dark-skinned men. Bee and her daughter argued constantly about that.

"You are young, smart and pretty," Bee said. "You have plenty of time for men, but when you get one, make sure he has good looks to complement yours. The worst thing you can do is bring me a bunch of grandchildren that look like little black-eyed peas."

So, when she saw Easter kissing Starkey Williams at the County Fair, Bee lost her sense of reason. She yanked Easter's arm and practically dragged her home, fussing and cussing all the way.

"Dammit, your father and I want better for you," she said. "That boy is no good. People *that* black don't even think the way we do. He will pump you full of babies and then run off to the next one. You stay away from him. You hear?"

It was October of 1918. The strong wind and the chill of the night predicted an early winter. And the rain. It had rained every day that week. Buckets and buckets of water had poured from the skies, strong enough to uproot the sweet potatoes. Bee rushed her daughter into the cold, damp house and pushed her down into a chair.

"I have to make a fire. You sit there and don't you move."

"Mama, I didn't do anything."

"But you were going to. I know from whence cometh that seed. You smelling your musk. I know it. You just like your grandma. The blacker the better."

Easter pouted and squirmed in her seat. She was mad as hell. For the first time in her life she felt anger and hatred towards her mother. She tuned her out and ignored the sound of "Easter!" Then again. "Eastaaah! Are you listening to me?"

Easter turned her back and focused on Starkey, handsome and smiling in his Army uniform. And with every exaggerated breath, every cold, rolled eye, her desire for him increased.

Bee was shaking with anger. She emptied the ashes from the stove and threw them out the back door. Then she placed brown paper bags at the bottom of the stove and went outside to get some wood. After loading it, she poured kerosene into the open gap and, as she shivered from the cold and her own emotions, she spilled the kerosene on her skirt. The wood was wet, so when she struck the match and tossed it onto the waiting pile, only the paper burned. The fire seemed to die out on purpose. Bee fumbled with another match and another, but it was no use; the fire would not start. She was filled with rage, and she trembled from the power of it. She emptied the kerosene jug into the stove, only this time, when she threw in the lighted match, there was a large explosion. Bee stumbled backwards. Her skirt was on fire. She fought the flames with all she had, beating at them with her fists and calling her daughter for help. When Easter finally turned around, she saw that her mother was a human torch. She ran outside to get water and Bee followed her. Easter had to prime the spigot to make the water flow, but by this time, Bee had reached the cabbage patch. She kept running, flailing her arms and moving her feet. And the screaming....

Easter realized that there was nothing she could do, so she watched in horror as her mother danced her way into eternity.

Part Three

Easter

Eleven

Now an orphan, Easter lived alone in the big house on the outskirts of Wilson. Starkey came to visit from time to time, just to keep her company. She was amazed at how much work was involved in keeping up a house and yard, and Starkey was eager to help her. He once brought her a goose that he thought she would prepare for Sunday dinner, but Easter made a pet of her and named her Bertha. The goose seemed to recognize her difference in the yard, and she held her head high in a regal manner as she strutted past the chickens.

Bertha was Easter's only friend when Starkey was away. She talked to her, sought advice from her, and she made her decisions based upon her interpretation of Bertha's *honk.*

In spite of her good sense, Easter found herself in love with Starkey. She did not want to disrespect the memory of her mother, but she didn't want to live the rest of her life with only a goose as company, either. With increasing enthusiasm, she looked forward to Starkey's visits. She planned around them. Lived for them. So, when Starkey got out of the Army and proposed marriage to her, she accepted after consulting with Bertha.

They were married in Wilson on March 19, 1919. The Army had taught Starkey nothing. He did not fight in the war, and he never traveled past Fort Bragg. But the uniform had helped him get the woman of his dreams, and he had to find a way to provide for her. There was a virus going around that was killing hundreds of people. Starkey wanted to protect Easter from coming in contact with people who had it.

Farming was all he knew. He found employment as a sharecropper, and he moved Easter to a house deep in the country behind an elementary school in Sharpsburg. They worked side by side on the farm, planting tobacco and corn, working the land the way God had intended. They were a solid pair, but Easter was very possessive. There was a time when a woman worker on the farm attempted to flirt with Starkey, and Easter flashed her a look with lightning in her eyes. The woman raised her hands in surrender and backed away. Seeing this, Starkey tried to calm the situation.

"Aw...c'mon, Baby. That woman's been wit' every man here. You think I want that?"

"Oh, I know what you want. And I know what you gon' get if you mess with her."

"What you saying?"

"You'll find out. Just try it."

"You don't have to worry 'bout that. I'm just as happy as a pig in slop."

"Yeah, you better be."

They hugged and went back to work. But she had firmly established her position as Mrs. Starkey Williams, and there was no question and no doubt about that.

There were three things that Easter loved aside from Starkey. She loved Bertha, she loved her snuff, and she *loved* her stump hole whiskey. Yes, she did. Like her mother before her, she called it white lightning, and she often tried to get Starkey to take a little nip. "C'mon, Shug. Just take a li'l bit with me." But he was not a drinking man. Besides, he sensed that Easter liked to fight. Somebody had to keep a cool head.

She also loved to dance. Starkey didn't care much for

dancing, but he would take her down to the juke joint in the holler and watch her dance by herself. He was a whole foot taller than she, and when her appetite for dancing was sated, he'd pick her up and carry her home.

The babies started coming right away: Dick in 1920, Molly in 1921, and Wiley in 1922. Easter stopped working the fields so she could take care of them. Their baby boy was the color of sand, and he had a head full of curly hair. Easter favored him, indeed, and that's when the arguments started. Starkey wanted her to divide her love equally among their children, but Easter would melt at that cute little face and wavy hair.

They began to fight over nothing, over *everything.* He complained that the iced tea was lukewarm. She complained that there was not enough money to buy ice.

"You spend money on the wrong things," he said.

"You don't make enough money for me to spend on anything," she said.

"I provide for my family!"

"Yeah...until your money runs out. But when we need coffee and sugar, who goes to get it when you don't have money? Me! I'm the provider! I'm the one who makes a way when there ain't none! Got me out here in this dump. I got a nice house in Wilson. We should have stayed there!"

He hauled off and slapped her face. She sailed onto him like a wild cat. He tried to fling her off of him, but she put her hands around his throat and dug her nails into his flesh.

Starkey learned that day that he could not whip Easter. He learned that quickly. She fought him like a man, and anything close was a convenient weapon—the scrub board, a frying pan full of eggs—she would use everything she had to keep him from beating her. When they were both bleeding and exhausted, Starkey went to sit on the front porch. Easter went back to her household duties.

So, this one day in 1931, Wiley wanted to walk to

the road. It was a Sunday, and all the children loved to get to Highway 301 on Sundays in hopes of seeing a car. Most folks still used horses and buggies as a means of transportation, and seeing a car lifted the spirits of the boys. It was a promise of a better future. A lifestyle of riding *in* something rather than on it. It didn't have to be fed or watered in quite the same way as a horse, and it didn't have to be cleaned up after, either. But Wiley was too young to go by himself, and Dick refused to go with him. Wiley went crying to his mother who, in turn, whipped Dick with a tobacco stick. Starkey was absolutely furious.

Easter was frying fish when he charged at her. "How you gon' put a stick on my firstborn son?"

"That boy been slouching around here all day. He needed a whipping."

"Why didn't you tell me? I'm his daddy!"

"And I'm his mama! Or don't that count?"

"You talking crazy, woman. You just mad 'cause your precious little Wiley didn't get his way!"

Easter threw the pan of hot grease at Starkey. He ducked, and the grease hit the table and the walls. It smeared all over the floor. Starkey took off running, slipping and sliding in the grease, running on his hands and knees. A week passed before he came back.

Starkey didn't cuss. Good thing. Easter had a wide vocabulary of cuss words. Every once in a while he would say something completely unintelligible: *dag gum boy, bum swiggle,* and that helped him get through the turmoil that Easter would start without warning. That was the hard part. He never knew what to expect of her. They could be walking along the path to or from the house and holding hands when all of a sudden, she'd lash out at him for no reason. He never knew why she was so angry; he always tried to please her. Even when Bertha disappeared Starkey tried to be there for her. But Easter would have none of it. She accused him directly of being jealous of the bird. He must have given her away. Bertha would never just wander off like that.

The tension in their house was unbearable and in 1934 it all came to a head. Starkey complained about her lack of diligence as a wife. She never denied him, but lately she had been simply present in their bedroom activities—no real participation at all. They argued about that. "Some things need to change around here. When I try to love you, you just lay there. And you don't keep this house clean worth a bum swiggle. You better straighten up, girl."

"You can't expect to poke a hole in me every night and then have me cook and clean all day. Hell, I'm tired."

And then one day Easter fried some fish and served it with biscuits. Starkey complained again.

"What's got into you, girl?"

"What do you mean?"

"You 'sposed to make cornbread with fish."

That's all it took. She said nothing, but she gave him a look that should have warned him that he would pay for that comment.

It had been a long, hot day of hard work. Starkey took off his clothes and shoes and went to bed. He fell asleep quickly, and he dreamed about beef. Large chunks of trembling, bloody beef, steaming in the cool of the evening after its slaughter. He smelled the blood, strong and close, and it caused him to stir. He awoke to find Easter straddled him. She held a butcher knife in her hand, and there was a slit across his face that trailed down towards his jugular. He did not move. Didn't make a sound. His eyes told the story of his terror.

Easter said, "Next time you want to criticize my cooking, you just remember this night. Ya hear?"

Starkey left that night and never returned. Easter moved back to her house in Wilson.

With the dissolution of the marriage, the children were left to fend for themselves like newly weaned puppies or fledglings when the nest becomes too small.

The surrounding neighbors tried to step in and give

guidance they believed the children needed. At the time Dick was fourteen, Molly was thirteen and Wiley was twelve. They stayed alone in the house, and for a while, it worked well. Both Molly and Wiley could cook, so the local wives made sure they had plenty of whatever they needed to survive. Of course, these gift givers saw themselves as charitable, and they constantly reminded the Williams family that they were indeed in their debt and needed to show some gratitude. The neighbors expected small favors in return—a cord of chopped wood, some free babysitting, or help with harvesting whatever was ready at the time.

For the most part the Williams trio obliged. They were grateful to have someone who cared enough to see that they ate. But Wiley hated farm work. His mother had never made him do it. His skin was perfect, and she did not want to see his hands covered with dirt and blisters any more than he did. So, while Dick and Molly worked the farm, Wiley hunted rabbits, squirrels. and birds. He had a natural gift for cooking, and he proudly presented to his siblings whatever he had bagged that day.

A man came galloping into the yard one day when Wiley was skinning a rabbit on the porch steps.

"Where yo' brother and sister?" he demanded.

"They in the house."

"Well go get 'em!"

"What for?"

"Old man Lassiter's barn is on fire. We need every hand we can get!"

"Y'all go 'head. I'm busy."

"Boy, did you hear what I said? The man's barn is burning down! I need you to hand some water. Now move your ass!"

Wiley eyed his shotgun that was propped against the porch. He called his family.

"Dick, Molly! Y'all better come out here and talk to this man."

The man dismounted his horse and strode towards Wiley. "I don't know who you think you are, boy. But you gon' come with me or I'll take the skin off your hide."

With that he rushed towards Wiley. Dick and Molly made it to the porch just in time to see Wiley swing his shotgun like a baseball bat. The blow landed at the man's temple. He was dead before he hit the ground.

For a moment everybody stood completely still. They didn't even breathe. Then all at once they panicked. The blood gushed from the man's skull like a faucet. Wiley's words of self-defense died in his throat. "Oh shit...oh shit!" was all he could say.

They all started running. They ran all the way to the road. When they got there, they stopped to rest. They hugged and without a word, each of them went in different directions. Molly went to Sharpsburg, Dick went to Elm City, and Wiley went to Wilson. It took him two days to make it.

●

Wiley knew the dangers of a colored boy alone at night, so he traveled by day and slept in trees when it got dark. He ate roots and berries, and he chewed sour grass when he could not find water. He had brought his shotgun with him, but just before he reached Wilson, he threw it in the creek.

The cook at the Do Drop Inn didn't know what to make of the dirty, raggedy, sleeping boy he found behind the restaurant. He must be lost, he thought—a dangerous situation for a colored boy in 1934, especially here in the South. For a while he just stared at the child, watching him take long, audible breaths. Fearing that he would draw attention to himself by being absent from the kitchen too long, he decided to wake the boy and hear his story. When he slapped Wiley on the leg, the child jumped up with his fists raised.

"Whoa, soldier," the cook said, raising the palms of his hands.

"Who are you?"

"My name is Jones. I'm the cook at this fine establishment."

Wiley nodded.

"What you doing out here, boy?"

"Well, I *was* sleeping."

"Oh I could see that. Why don't you go home to sleep?"

"Ain't got no home."

"Where yo' people?"

"Ain't got no people, neither."

"Well, what's yo' plan? You can't stay here forever."

"Figured I'd find me a job somewhere. Get my own place."

The cook gazed at Wiley curiously. "How old are you, boy?"

"Twelve."

"Twelve, huh? What can you do at twelve? Why ain't you in school?"

"I don't read good." He quickly added, "But I can cook. I'm pretty good at that."

"You got a name?"

"Oh, yes, suh. It's Wiley. Wiley Williams, suh."

"Well come on in here. Let's get you cleaned up. You hungry?"

"Yes, suh. Thank you, Mr. Jones."

Jones grimaced. "Ah, Wiley...don't call me 'Mr.' in here. The white folks don't like that. Jones will do."

"Yes, suh."

Jones led Wiley to a broom closet and gave him a white uniform. He wet a rag and handed it to the child. "Here. Wash yo' face and put these on. I'll talk you up to the boss." He handed Wiley a plate of bacon, eggs, and grits. "Don't you worry none. It'll be all right."

Sure enough, when the boss came, Jones said to him, "Mr. Charlie, this here is my nephew, Wiley. He wants to learn the cooking business. So, I told him to come help me out for a spell. You...you don't have to pay him nothing, yet. Let's just see how he works out. Okay, Sir?"

Charlie glared at the child briefly. "It's okay with me," he said. Long as he doesn't break anything. He looks kinda young."

Jones smiled broadly. "Oh yes, Sir. That's the best

time to get 'em. Okay if he sleep in the broom closet? That way he'll be here on time for breakfast, Sir."

Charlie nodded his consent. Now Wiley had a job and a place to stay.

The next day there was a small article in *The Wilson Daily Times* about a colored man who was apparently thrown from his horse and landed on his head against the steps of an abandoned house. Because the body had begun to decompose, they buried him quickly.

Twelve

EASTER'S HOUSE WAS UNCOMFORTABLE. SHE TRIED TO BLAME it on her circumstance. She was alone. Bertha was gone. Starkey was gone. And she had left her children when she returned to Wilson. She had told them that she needed to fix the place up some, but when she tried to go back for them, they were not to be found.

The house was in disrepair. After being empty for so long, she had come back to mold and mildew on the walls, rats in the pantry, and she even found a snake nesting in her bedroom.

But the biggest problem with the house was that it held haunting memories of her mother. Bee's death had started right there in the front room, and Easter simply could not get that image out of her mind. Every time she entered the room it was right there in her face, bold and accusing. She kept herself busy during the day, but the night folded in on her like a shroud, smothering her and daring sleep to come. So, when she thought she saw her mother slip quietly past her open door, Easter knew it was time to go.

She put a sign on her front yard and, because of the huge property, the house sold immediately. Three thousand dollars. Enough to buy another house with no history. She found a spot on Wiggins Street. The kitchen was on the front of the house with a window that faced the street. There was a large, open room, flanked by three smaller rooms on each side, an inside toilet, and a backyard big enough for a garden. The house itself sat on cinder blocks, so there was room to crawl under it in case there was a problem with the plumbing.

Easter moved into her new house with big plans. She would find her children and bring them to live with her. She could start some kind of business—cooking or sewing or maybe taking in laundry. There was no lack of talent in Easter. She had worked all her life and believed she could do anything. Among her gifts, and perhaps the best of them all, was her ability to cook. She could turn anything into a fine meal and her specialty was fried fish. Visitors, folks at the fair or at church, all praised her for her fried porgies. Her secret lay in the seasonings she used in her batter: salt, black pepper, a little garlic and just a hint of cayenne. She used lard and a deep skillet, deep enough to cover both sides of the fish at one time.

When Easter cooked, the aroma traveled into the street and her neighbors took notice. A woman from across the street sauntered in one day and said, "I just come to see what in the world you are cooking!" Easter invited her to a meal, and the neighbor, in turn, told everyone she knew about Easter's culinary talents. Within a few weeks of living on Wiggins Street she had established a Friday night business of selling fish dinners in her community. At first it was just food: fried fish, Cole slaw, stewed potatoes, and cornbread. Her clients would pick up their meals and take them back to their own homes. But then they started to ask for drinks and, just as easily, they asked to sit down and eat while the food was still hot.

She started to pay attention to her profits. Fish were easy to get; there was a fish market on Goldsboro Street and very often the men in the community would bring her the freshwater fish they caught by the bushels. It was like that. Fresh vegetables, freshly killed hogs, huge bags of peanuts for roasting, a chicken here and there, and a couple dozen brown eggs—whatever they had they would bring for Easter to cook and sell. She bought potatoes in twenty-five pound bags for $2.50. She purchased gallon sized jugs of corn liquor for five dollars each, and she sold it at fifty cents a shot. She was making good money. Her clients felt good in her home. People didn't mind giving because she gave so much in return. They laughed and talked, smoked and played cards, talked and lingered for long periods of time, and Easter was the boss.

She worked all day long on Fridays and well into the early morning hours of Saturdays, but she realized that it was not enough to build the empire she had hoped to achieve. She would have to get to know better the folks in her new surroundings. She would have to think about what their needs were. Her father had taught her to study her clients and to figure out how to best serve them. She had to think about the kind of business that would be long-lasting. She had to think...*think*....

Pussy! Now that was a commodity that had a large consumer base and it would never go out of style. She could sell pussy. Not hers, of course, but she could convince other women to sell theirs and make themselves some money in the process.

It was not difficult to expand her list of clients; men thought Easter was attractive and she was very friendly— flirtatious, even. The men often propositioned her and, figuring that they could not afford her, they teased about putting a little piece on layaway or an installment plan. "It might be too much for me," one man said. "But I'll try anything once."

And Easter teased right back. "You can't handle all this, little boy." But she gave up nothing. Instead, she was able to find a few young girls who needed a little help feeding their babies or getting their hair done. The price list was simple: three dollars for flat back; two dollars to blow his pipe, and a dollar for a hand job. Easter took fifty percent. She was open every day, and in less than a month she was averaging more than seventy dollars a week.

So, that's how Easter Cooper Williams became the madam of Wiggins Street. Her brothel became more popular than any other colored business in town. She continued to sell corn liquor for fifty cents a shot, and fried fish plates for a dollar, but these were her cover and protection from the police. The money poured in, and her business grew. Her life was filled with music and laughing people. Every once in a while, she would have one of her moments of unpredictable rage and make them all leave her house, but in time they all came to know that about her and, after giving her a chance to cool off, they would all saunter back into the same routine.

Everyone in town knew Easter's real business. Women in general, and married women in particular, all knew that Easter was the go-to woman if they were looking for their man, but they did not dare approach her. She was armed always, and she was dangerous. Always. So they tried to pretend that she did not exist. They joined church and prayed for her. They joined forces and prayed for their men. But Easter had a winning smile and a power that could not be whetted.

Her power over her girls was evident; Easter could make arrangements that they themselves lacked the courage to do. Her power over the men was a little tricky and more solid. Because she would not give herself to them, they admired her. She was the forbidden fruit that all the men sought, but none of them reaped.

So, it surprised her and her customers when Dave Evans strolled into her house early one Sunday morning in 1942. It was actually the pitiful remains of Saturday night, and the last couple was just finishing their rendezvous. Dave was tall and black. He had a guitar strapped around his back and huge, white teeth. One of them was wrapped in gold and, after removing his hat he said to her, "Mornin,' Ma'am. I'm new in town and hungry. I hear tell that you fry a pretty mean fish."

Easter giggled like a girl. "Indeed, I do," she said. "Set yo'self down and rest a spell. What brings you to Wilson?"

"I'm looking for work. Word has it that they are hiring over at the rock quarry."

Dave played his guitar while Easter cooked. He strummed a simple melody before he started to sing "God Bless the Child." His voice was smooth and sweet. Easter hummed along and swayed to his music while she prepared his meal.

He was pleased with what he saw: a pretty little fat thing who enjoyed her role of serving a man. He could tell that she knew how to handle her business. His flashy smile, his beautiful sable-colored skin, and his velvety voice made her squeeze her thighs together as she delivered his plate. He said, "Thanky, Ma'am. I *sho nuff prechate* it."

They were in love before the sun rose.

•

Wiley grew into a tall and handsome young man. He had grace and charm. He developed a reputation for making the best over easy egg in the county, and the patrons of the Do Drop Inn often sent a tip for him to the kitchen. The boss loved his work. Wiley would set the tables before he started cooking. He'd place the forks and knives next to the plates, put a flower or candle on each table as a center piece, and he folded the napkin in such a way that it looked like the Pope's mitre.

The dining room was large, and each table was covered with a white cloth. There was a window behind the cash register, so the diners could see Wiley as he prepared their food. Every so often he'd catch someone staring at him and, depending upon the gender of that person, he would part his wide lips that were partially hidden under his thick moustache. It was always men who received this gift. Jones had warned him that there was no future in smiling at white women. Whenever he caught their eye, he politely nodded and continued his work.

He was as close to happy as one could get. He worked for good white folks, people who appreciated the way he improved their business. On payday Mr. Charlie generally gave him two dollars extra. By 1942, he had his own little spot in which to live, a room at Mrs. Ellis' boarding house. And Wiley had become the head cook; Jones was *his* assistant.

He bought himself a couple of Zoot suits, a pocket watch, and a fedora with a long feather. He also bought a bicycle—red with white-rimmed tires. It had a luggage rack on the back and a tooter on the front. On occasion he would take some girl for an ice cream cone, and he was often fortunate enough to take her to his place for the night. Women loved him. They threw themselves at him at the juke joint. They even fought over the privilege to be with him. So, he had choices—plenty of them, and because none of them quite fit into his criteria of being just right, he had no problem with going home alone.

His bicycle served as a rite of passage. The guy with the prettiest bike got the prettiest girl. Plain and simple. He took care of his bike very well by washing and waxing it every weekend. He made sure the tires were scrubbed clean, and he bought little ribbons for the handlebars. Wiley proudly rode through the streets of Wilson on the prowl, surely, for fresh meat, yet trying not to be obvious.

One day in July of 1943 he rode through Viola Street. It was a mistake because the street was unpaved, and he had just detailed his bike. But once he made the left turn off of Reid Street he was totally committed to follow through. It was a Sunday, and he was in a show off mood. A girl sat barefoot on a front porch. He waved. She waved and smiled. He felt his heart jump, but he continued down the street. He did, however, take note of the number on the door: 802. He crossed Vick Street and, as he climbed the hill to make his way towards Pender, he knew he would come back and casually make some excuse for stopping. So, he turned around at Elba and went back to where he saw her. She was no longer on the porch.

The disappointment made his ride home a long one, but he determined to take the trip again on his next day off.

And he did. The girl was nowhere to be found, so this time he stopped at Sherrod Grocery, the store that was next to her house. Inside he saw a light-skinned young man with grey eyes who was in the throes of a sneezing fit. His face was red, and he sneezed more than a dozen times. Wiley looked around the store while he waited for the man to recover. There was a drink box just to the left of the entrance. The shelves were loaded with cereal, sugar, washing powder and bleach. At the back of the store was a tub of pickled pig feet. Across the end was a heater, the chimney pipe extending through the roof. On the right was a table with a large round of hoop cheese. The shelves on that side held mayonnaise, mustard, ketchup, potted meat, soda crackers and canned sardines. Behind the counter were all kinds of cigars and loose cigarettes, and on the counter sat gallon jugs of dill and sour pickles, two-for-a-penny cookies and candy, snuff and chewing tobacco. Wiley ordered a White Owl cigar.

The man took his handkerchief from his back pocket and wiped his eyes and mouth. "Sorry 'bout that sneezing," the store owner said. "Got hay fever bad. Ain't seen you around here before. New in town?"

His voice was very loud, like he was hard of hearing or something. So, Wiley spoke loudly, too, and he leaned towards the man. "Naw, not really. Just new to this area."

"Why are you yelling?"

"'Cause I thought you were."

"This ain't yelling. This just talking."

Wiley smiled. "Oh...okay. Name's Wiley Williams."

"Nice to meet you," the man shouted. "My name is Solomon Sherrod, Jr. But folks 'round here call me Shird."

They shook hands. Shird handed him the cigar and Wiley gave up a nickel.

"Ah, Shird...you know anything about the folks next door?"

"Li'l bit. That's my house."

Wiley's eyes lit up like celestial beings. "Well, I passed through here last week and I saw a pretty girl sitting on your front porch. You happen to know who that might be?"

"Probably my little sister Beulah. She too young for you. She ain't but sixteen."

"When she gonna be seventeen?"

"March."

"Oh. Guess I better wait, then. No matter. I was just curious is all."

That was a lie. It was more than curiosity that drove him to learn more about her. She was young and innocent looking. She was beautiful. She had features like the Tuscarora Indians that used to dominate that area, and she had long, silky, straight hair. Beulah fit the image he had created in his mind of the girl who would become his wife. And to think he had to wait a whole year for her was almost too much to bear.

His thoughts of Beulah began to interfere with his work. He burned bacon while he stood at the stove daydreaming about her. The customers complained that the tables were not set properly. The toast was dry, or the grits were lumpy. He would take long walks on his break and forget to go back to work. After a while, when Charlie saw the need to address the issue, Wiley told him, "I can't stay here no more. I got other things to do."

The truth is he thought he was losing his mind over want of Beulah. He couldn't focus on anything but her. So, he reasoned that if he could get away, he could find something else to do with his life. Maybe he'd forget all about her. Or, maybe traveling would help him endure the wait.

The country was at war, so Wiley joined the Army. He knew he would not be able to fight, but he gladly signed on to cook. After taking all the medical tests, he prepared to ship out immediately. By now both Dick and Molly had moved to Wilson, and each of them was married and had children. Wiley left his bike at Dick's house. He put a tarp over it and dared Dick to touch it. The bike would be safe and available to attract Beulah when he returned to Wilson. Dick assured him of this.

He made it through boot camp without a hitch. When he got back to Wilson, he was on a mission to find two women: the one who had killed his heart when she left him and the one who had brought it back to life.

Finding his mother was not difficult. The first person he visited was Dick. With only a few days free, he needed to get his bike so he could get around faster. The brothers greeted each other with smiles, handshakes, and a short bout of Jiu Jitsu. It was a ritual they shared when they were children. This, coupled with a few fake Joe Louis punches and shouts of "Watch out there now!" showed that the bond between them was still intact.

"Have you seen Mama?" Wiley asked.

"Yeah. She lives on Wiggins Street, near Daniel Hill. You going over there?"

"First thing."

"Okay. Be careful. She always has a house full of company."

"Company?"

Dick winked. "You know."

"Oh…is that right?"

"She's making plenty of money. I know she will be glad to see you. She's been asking about you." He stared at his brother's eyes. "How you doing?"

Wiley moved his hand down the side of his uniform. "How I look?"

Dick laughed. "You look good."

"See there? You answered your own question."

•

Daniel Hill was an area of Wilson that was far away from the active, colored community. It was on the south side of town near the white settlement, but it was isolated, indeed, almost like an island. It was predominantly filled with old, cheap, one-family dwellings that were rented by colored folks. Some of the houses had dirt floors. None of the streets were paved, but it was a very self-contained community. There was a store, a pool hall, an elementary school and, of course, it was close to Easter's Speak Easy for entertainment. The only thing missing was a high school, so the teenagers who lived there had to walk the two miles to get to Darden High.

Most of the men who lived there were employed at Center Brick warehouse or Export Tobacco Factory. A few worked at the quarry. Some were mechanics or shoeshine boys or elevator operators at Cherry Hotel in uptown Wilson. There were a few janitors at Carolina General Hospital, local schools, and the drive-in movie. Still others did odd jobs and day work. They would stand on the corner of Hines and Pender Streets and wait for the driver of a pick-up truck, any pickup truck to stop and offer them work. Daniel Hill was convenient to uptown; it was just a short walk to Belk-Tyler, Branch Banking and Trust, and the County Courthouse.

Like any good business person, Easter kept a keen eye on what was happening in Wilson and the surrounding areas. Great changes were taking place and Easter, ever aware of them, was constantly adjusting and thinking about how those changes would affect her. At this point, for example, people would go to the General Store and give the clerk a list of the things they wanted to buy. But somebody had come up with an idea that Easter thought was brilliant. Grocery stores were being built all through the South where folks could go in and shop for themselves. Some of the stores were called Winn-Dixie and some were Piggly Wiggly and A&P. They were equipped with baskets and wheeled carts, and people would take the merchandise off the shelves themselves. In that way they could compare prices of different brands, read ingredients, and make their own choices. According to the newspapers, plans were in progress to bring such a store to Wilson. This meant more jobs for colored people. Somebody had to scrub floors and stock the shelves. With new jobs came new money for her. Easter thought it was a masterful idea. By now the Coca-Cola plant had located in Wilson and she was beside herself with joy over the growth of the little town.

Easter's business remained the center of her community. It attracted men from Daniel Hill, from the east side of town, and sometimes men came from as far away as Rocky Mount. They all, in turn, told everyone they knew about it. She had clients for miles around her, and Wiley recognized that fact right away.

It was only ten o'clock in the morning when he rounded the corner to his mother's street. He could hear the music and loud laughter. The scent of fish frying drifted to his nostrils and lingered there. He parked his bike near the steps and, while the door stood wide open, he felt the need to knock. He heard his mother coming long before he saw her. It was the familiar sound of her slippers slapping the bottoms of her feet as she walked. That was one thing he would never forget about her, and when she did appear, the two of them stood gazing at each other with unasked questions loitering around in their heads.

She was a little bit chubbier than he remembered. And shorter. Her hair, parted down the middle with braids that fell softly down her chest, had begun to gray just around her temples. Her mouth was full of snuff, and as she wiped her hands on her apron, her eyes grew larger and larger with recognition.

"Wiley?" she said. And then again, "Wiley!" She jumped into the arms of her baby boy and hugged him. He lifted her off her feet and swung her around on the front porch. Finally, she said, "Put me down. Let me get a good look at you."

Wiley lowered his mother to the floor, took off his cover, and turned slowly to display himself.

"My, my, my! What a handsome fella you turned out to be. Come on in here and meet everybody."

Easter took her son by the hand and led him into the large room. It had become a kind of lobby where her customers waited their turn for a vacant spot. She introduced Wiley to the crowd of patrons. One of the men said, "Boy... you born for good luck. You look your mama's face!" And another said, "Just look *atcha*. Ain't nothing but legs and shoulders." They all laughed and continued with their merriment. Easter made Wiley welcome to try any of her *products* for free, but he declined, claiming that he had to report for duty early the next morning. So, she handed him a breakfast of fish and grits and took him to the back porch.

"I was so worried about you. How you been?"

"Oh. I'm all right."

"Well, what have you been doing? It's been damn near ten years since I saw you last."

"You mean since you left me?"

"Now you listen here, boy. You don't know the shit I had to put up with, so don't come in here accusing me. I had to leave. I had to find a way to feed you and your brother and sister after your sorry ass daddy left."

"You never came back."

"I did, too! Y'all were gone and I couldn't find you anywhere."

"Maybe you didn't look hard enough. I was working at the Do Drop Inn for a long time before I went into the Army."

"Humph. I haven't been on the east side of town since I sold my house."

"It don't matter, Mama. I guess I turned out all right."

"Yes, you did. I'm so proud of you, son."

He finished his breakfast and handed the plate to her. "I gotta go. I'll come to see you again next time I'm in town."

"You be sure to do that. You're always welcome here."

She walked him to the front porch and Wiley hopped astride his bike and left. He rode straight to Viola Street. He whistled the entire way. As he parked his vehicle next to the stop sign at Vick Street he started to sing "Stormy Monday Blues." And could that boy ever sing! He had a deep, baritone voice like Billy Eckstein, and Wiley knew all of Eckstein's songs. He walked slowly, trying to be nonchalant, and pretending to be doing something other than hoping to see Beulah. He spotted her on the back porch. She was washing clothes and hanging them on the line to dry. Their eyes met and, as he stood there serenading her, she fell off the porch and knocked herself unconscious. For many years Wiley would tell his children and grandchildren about this day. "I was so purty...she took one look at me in my uniform and fainted dead away." He'd throw his head back and laugh as if it had just happened, and then he'd repeat, "I was so purty!"

Beulah recalled the scene differently. She would say, "I didn't faint. I fell. I tripped over the rinse bucket."

Either way, he ran to lift her from the ground, and they both instantly knew that they were destined to live the rest of their lives together. It was just one month after her seventeenth birthday.

Thirteen

Sometimes people who are the exact opposite are drawn to each other the way lightning is attracted to water. The mystery of their differences is what makes them who they are. It has a way, this difference, of feeding on itself, bubbling and growing until it erupts in volcanic fashion and spreads over everyone involved. At times it is amiable, and it complements and nurtures all parties involved. Other times it is capable of destruction, and it causes little fissures that remain in the heart festering wider and wider until the gap opens like a chasm beyond repair.

Such was the relationship between Easter and Dave. They were complete opposites. She, for example, was forty-two; he was twenty-eight. She was five feet four; he was over six feet tall. She was almost white in color; he was darker than ebony. Easter was loud, quick-tempered, and full of fire. Dave was like cool running water.

It was, perhaps, this difference that kept them together. She saw him as a necessity in her business. He would work at the quarry all day long and then come home in the evening to help her keep order because, of course, there were sometimes fights. The patrons respected Dave, and they rarely became unruly when he was present. This was quite a feat because by now, some of the clients were white men. At first it caused a stir. The colored men resisted such an invasion of their territory. But Dave assured them that money is money, and the whites were willing to pay more. Easter invented a way to make everyone comfortable. She doubled the prices for the white men and all her previous clients assumed that they were getting a "colored man's discount."

But things started to change again in May of 1944, when a white woman came to Easter's house looking for work. Easter answered the door with her usual response from the kitchen.

"Come on in. Door's open."

She stopped her work abruptly when she saw the cute, young woman standing in her lobby. "Can I help you?" she asked as she took inventory of the girl: a pretty face, long blond hair, and a round, watermelon ass like a colored girl.

"Why, yes Ma'am. I'm looking for Miss Easter."

"Well, you found me. What do you want? You a bill collector?"

"Oh, no, Ma'am." Seeing all the wide-eyed people staring at her she said, "Could I speak with you in private?"

Easter led the girl to the back porch.

"My name is Mary. I have heard about you, and I was hoping you would be willing to give me a job."

"Are you crazy?"

"No, Ma'am."

"Do you know the kind of business I run?"

"Yes, Ma'am."

"Then why did you come here?"

"My mama's ailing. I need a lot of money to pay for her care."

"No...I mean, why did you come *here?* Ain't they got no whorehouses in your neck of the woods?"

"Yes, Ma'am."

"Why don't you go to one of them?"

"I don't want anybody to know."

Easter chuckled. Well, I guess I understand that. You got any diseases?"

"No, Ma'am."

Easter folded her arms and cupped her chin, pretending to be thinking about Mary's proposal. The truth is she saw dollar signs when she first laid eyes on the girl. "When do you want to start?"

"I'm ready now."

So, Easter led Mary into the house and introduced her to the waiting crowd.

"Everybody, this is our new girl. Her name is Mary."

A white man looked at Mary and quickly voiced his disapproval. "Humph!" he said. "White trash."

And Mary said, "Yo' mammy was!"

With that Easter knew that her decision to hire Mary was the right thing to do. White men came to her place to be with colored girls, but they despised the notion that white girls would willingly give themselves to colored men. The colored men, on the other hand, felt a kind of retribution. Their women had historically been exposed to whites imposing themselves upon them, but the white woman was off limits. Now, they could balance that equation and enjoy white flesh without punishment. It was a perfect solution to an age-old frustration.

Dave was uneasy. "You just asking for trouble," he said.

"Well, let's just give it a few days. See how it works out. Plenty *niggers* around here want to try out a white woman. She can bring in a lot of money."

Mary entertained four clients that day, and as Easter handed her twelve dollars in commission, she promised to return the next day. Each day she stayed longer and earned more, and eventually she was being paid more than Easter's number one whore. This caused resentment among the colored girls, and while the men waited for their turn with Mary, some of them became impatient.

Easter and Dave were in the backyard talking when Mary ran out screaming. "Miss Easter! Miss Easter! They fighting!"

The fight had started between two men, but as it

progressed, others had joined in, and Dave and Easter ran into a full-blown free-for-all. They broke furniture and dishes, and they swore oaths of death to each other. Easter ran into her bedroom, and she returned with her shotgun. She fired a shot through the ceiling and all movement stopped. She reached into her pocket and reloaded the gun.

"Now, I'm going to say this one time. Go home...or somewhere and cool the fuck off. Don't come up in here with that shit again."

The men scattered like roaches. The women took the rest of the day off.

For the first time in over ten years Easter's house was free of guests. She felt uneasy, threatened, like maybe something else was coming. She didn't know what to do with herself, work was all she knew. But there was somehow a magical gift in the silence as she and Dave sat staring at each other. She exhaled loudly, and, expecting to find comfort and understanding in him, she walked over and sat on his lap.

"What the hell just happened?" she said to him.

He looked at her accusingly. "I told you that you shouldn't have brought that white woman in here. I told you."

She got up and moved to the couch. "Uh huh. You *told* me. You didn't seem to mind it so much when you were spending my money."

"Your money? Hell, woman. I work! I work every day at the quarry."

"Umm hmmm. Just look at you. You come home, take a bath for an hour and then slip into that fancy silk shirt you got on. That shirt cost more than you make in a week. In fact, I make more in a day than you make in a whole week."

"Well, at least it's good, honest work."

"And mine ain't? The way I see it, you got one job and one job only."

"Oh yeah? What is that?"

"You need to do what you do best. Just sit there and look cute. Stay out of grown folks' business."

"Easter, I am well past three times seven. Don't talk to me like I'm a child."

"I talk to you as I please. I got drawers older than you. And I say what I want to say in *this* house."

He rose from his seat and started towards her. Easter stood up, too.

"Make sure you know what you doing, now," she said. "I know that look. The last man who tried to beat me carries a scar across his face to this day. Be careful. This may not be what you want."

He paused for a moment. Then he brushed past her and went outside. She watched him pacing the yard, his teeth clenched, his fists pounding the air. He talked to someone or something invisible to Easter. Sweat beaded on his face and the back of his expensive shirt was wet down the middle. After a while he sat on the bench and put his face in his hands. She went to put the shotgun back into the bedroom.

Easter toyed with the idea of going to him. He looked spent, whipped, and she wanted to ease his pain. She chose instead to let him come to her. He was a little boy outfitted in a grown man's body. He needed to be taught a lesson. *She* was the boss of her house, and once his tantrum was over, he would come to his senses and realize that. She made dinner and called him in to eat. He walked slowly, reluctantly towards the house. When they sat at table she said to him, "You finished?"

"Finished what?"

"Pouting."

"I wasn't pouting."

"Really? What were you doing?"

"I was trying to calm down. I don't want to hurt you."

"I'm not worried about you hurting me. You got to bring ass to kick ass. Whatever you do to me I'm gonna give right back to you."

"You don't understand. The way you said 'this house'

made me feel like nothing. Like you were saying that if I didn't like the way things were around here I could go and you would find somebody else. That made me so goddamn mad...I could have *killed* you, girl."

"What part of that is a lie? You are free to go whenever you please."

"See, that's what I'm talking about. You act like you don't care nothing about me. All you do is work. Cooking and cleaning and hustling them girls. We never do anything together until it's time to go to bed."

"I am all about making money. If you ain't talking about money you wasting your time talking to me."

"Money ain't everything. We need to spend some time just having fun together."

"Doing what?" Her question was genuine. They did seem to be in a rut lately. Her schedule left no room for spontaneity; the house was usually full of people until closing time at two in the morning. Then they both hit the floor at eight to start their workday. It was a routine day in and day out that never altered and by the time they went to bed, well, their lovemaking was more habitual than passionate.

"We could go to the juke joint and have some fun with other people. Hell, I might even take my guitar. You can dance and I could play and sing. Folks would enjoy that I reckon."

She smiled. The look in his eyes was that of a child asking for a new toy. "When do you suggest we do that?"

In her smile he saw a break in her rigidness. It was an opening for him to get his way. "How about Sunday?" he said. "Even God took a break on Sunday."

"That's what they say."

"We could sleep late, make love all afternoon, and then go the joint to dance the night away. We could even go to church on Sunday morning."

She laughed out loud. "Uh uh...don't push it. You think God is gonna want a whore monger up in His house of worship?"

They both laughed then, and just as they started to relax a little, Easter asked him, "Where did you come from, Dave? Where's home?"

"Everywhere. Nowhere."

"What about your people? Your parents?"

"I never knew them. I was raised by my grandma."

"You married? Got any kids?"

"No. Next."

"Well, I just realized that I don't know a thing about you. I told you about how my daddy died. I told you about my mama. I told you what happened between me and my husband. You have even met my kids, and I don't know a thing about you except you just showed up one night. What's the big mystery?"

"No mystery. You know that I'm here. You know this is where I want to be. That's all there is to know and all you need to know. Can I have a piece of that blackberry pie?"

"Sure, but it'll cost you."

Thinking that she was hinting at making love, he smiled. "What's it gonna cost me?"

"You can start by fixing that hole." She pointed to the ceiling. As she rubbed her inner thigh, she said to him, "Then you can fix this one right here."

The smile evolved into roaring laughter, and she rose to serve him. He was closed tight as a coconut, she thought, but she would find a way to crack that shell and reach his inside. She *would*.

Part Four

Beulah

Fourteen

SHE WAS HER FATHER'S FAVORITE CHILD. THE BABY GIRL OF what had been thirteen children, Beulah was a feisty little thing with an interest in everything. Her father adored her. He instilled in her a love of reading good books and being a wordsmith, he taught her how to use words that other people did not understand. She read Shakespeare, John Donne and Chaucer. She could recite their works by heart; she was fluent in French, and she sang like an angel. She was a stellar student in school and, once when her father met a man who used a phrase he did not know, it was Beulah who explained it to him. In a conversation the man used the word, *whatnot.* He said, "I went home from church yesterday and I whatnot." The phrase confused Solomon Sherrod until Beulah told him that the man meant he piddled around doing miscellaneous chores.

Being an intellectual, Beulah was not fond of household tasks. She would stay up reading until late at night, and her father encouraged and protected her in her efforts. Her sister Flora would get up early and start breakfast. When Beulah awoke, she would go into the kitchen, pour herself a cup of coffee, and sit down to read something. She was in the eleventh grade at Darden High School. Her father insisted on seeing and signing her report card himself. He planned to send her to college, and he was willing to invest everything he had to make that happen. She was ambitious and charming—traits that would take her far beyond teaching French in a classroom. She called him *Papa*, and on the rare occasions that he found it necessary to scold her, she would say, "I love you Papa," and his heart would turn to mush.

Beulah had dreams and plans beyond Viola Street, beyond Wilson. She wanted to travel and see the entire world. She used to walk to visit her sister Minnie Bell on Railroad Street and, after a quick snack and talk (Minnie Bell was a great cook), she would walk along the railroad tracks to Nash Street. The oncoming train and the ringing of the gate bells were music to her. Occasionally, she would hop onto a freight car and ride it to Elm City. She had no inhibitions and no fear. When the train slowed as it approached town, Beulah would jump off and walk through the woods until she reached Highway 301. This was her wild adventure whenever she had restless, itchy feet. Her mother lived her whole life within five miles of her birthplace. Her father, however, had walked to Wilson from Terre Haut, Indiana. At least that's the story he told her when he tried to convince her to travel. So, she believed she had inherited her father's adventurous spirit, and seven miles from Elm City to Wilson was a temporary satisfaction of her desire to go *somewhere*.

She was creative, tricky and mischievous. She and her cousin Elma, for example, used to steal liquor from their uncle's stash. Moonshine, white lightning, stump hole whiskey, and corn liquor were all pretty much the same, and Uncle June Scott Artis kept plenty of it in gallon jugs in his barn. The girls would run to the cornfield and empty the jugs, and then they would replace the liquid with water. This was done in fun, and they had many a great laugh watching how "drunk" the consumers became on plain water.

Elma played the piano and Beulah sang. Often, they would put on a recital for their parents and neighbors. Of course, they performed the songs that were church worthy:

"The Lord's Prayer," "Jesus Keep Me Near the Cross," and "Holy, Holy, Holy." Their biggest secret, however, was that the girls loved to dance. On Sunday afternoons they could be found behind the barn on June Scott's farm. They danced to the sound of their own voices as they did the jitterbug, boogie-woogie, and the Charleston.

Then there was the time when an older cousin fell asleep in June Scott's parlor. His name was Lawrence, and he was huge. He always wore coveralls, even on Sunday. His thighs were so big, he could not cross his legs, so when he sat, his Brogans were a yard apart on the floor. He used to eat hardily, and drink corn liquor until he fell asleep, sometimes at the dinner table. But on this one day when he had at least made it to the parlor, Beulah and Elma noticed that his stomach rose and fell as he inhaled and exhaled. He snored loudly as he took in air, and there was a whistling sound when he released it. His mouth was wide open. The girls emptied a bottle of castor oil into his mouth and then hid behind a chair to watch what happened. Lawrence swallowed the thick liquid with a snort, and he woke up cussing. "G-G-G-G-ga-awwd-damn!"

Beulah and Elma ran outside and rolled in the dirt with laughter. They laughed until the tears flowed, and they had to hold their hurting sides.

But on the day that Beulah fell or fainted or whatever, her life changed forever. She had fought with Flora that morning over who would do the washing. The fight ended when Flora hit Beulah with a stick of stove wood, so Beulah gathered the dirty whites and the lye soap and headed for the back porch. Of all the duties involved in keeping a house clean, she hated laundry the most. She did not like the way the hot water and soap wrinkled her hands and made her nails break. She resented the fact that once breakfast was finished, Flora could sit and sew all day long. No. Beulah had other things she wanted to do. Important things. And while she scrubbed the linens, her mind concentrated on the kind of life her future promised when she finished high school. She dreamed of faraway places like Paris and Rome. Fancy dresses and interesting conversations. She saw herself having breakfast beneath *la tour Eiffel,* as she flirted with handsome, beret-wearing men.

As she stood there daydreaming about it, she heard the deep, melodious voice of Wiley Williams. The next thing she knew, she was on the ground looking up at the handsome young soldier. He laughed when he picked her up, not a mean laugh, but one full of love. She was embarrassed, he could tell.

"Are you all right? Did you hurt yourself?"

"I'm fine." She brushed the dirt off her clothes and pulled herself away from him.

"You sure, now?"

She looked dazed. Rattled. "I'm sure," she said, still brushing herself with her wet and soapy hands. She pouted a little and shifted from one foot to the other until she found a comfortable stance. She folded her arms behind her and looked up at the sky.

Wiley took inventory of her body. Tiny waist, wide hips, bow-legged at the knee. After a few brief, but awkward moments he said, "My name is Wiley."

"Beulah."

"Nice to meet you, Miss Beulah."

She nodded.

"You know...you are the prettiest young lady in this whole town, the prettiest I have ever met."

"Oh, I don't believe that." She blushed.

"Yes, you do." He wore a devilish smile as he placed his cigar in the corner of his mouth. "Would you like to go for a ride?"

"I have to ask Papa."

"Then why don't you go do that?"

She nodded again and backed away. As she turned to enter the house, he watched her walk. Even in her work smock he could see what he would later learn was called the Sherrod shuffle. Everyone in the family had that walk. It looked like her backbone slipped and disconnected from her pelvis with each step. On Shird it looked like a lazy stroll, but on Beulah the walk created an intense sensation in his groin.

Her father was not at home, but Wiley did not have to know that right now. Once she was in the house, she quickly groomed herself and found her navy blue shoes. She put on her nicest dress, dabbed some vanilla behind her ears, tied her life savings, fifty-two cents, in a handkerchief and walked out of the front door. Her father had taught her to never go anywhere without her own money.

Wiley lifted her to the luggage rack and they left. He bought her some ice cream, and they went to the Ritz Theater to see a movie—*Gaslight*—with Charles Boyer and Ingrid Bergman. Afterwards, he left his bike downtown and they walked hand in hand back to her house.

My cousin Elma and I want to be teachers," she told him. "She's a little bit older and she's in college already."

"Really? What do you want to teach?"

"French. My teacher, Mrs. Miller? She says I am a natural for it."

"Where do you plan to go? To college, I mean."

"NCC. It's in Durham."

"Oh. That's kinda far."

Seeing what she sensed as disappointment in his face she said, "Not too far. You can get there in about four or five hours by bus. Shird took me there once. My sister Aileen lives in Durham. What about you? What do you plan to do when you get out of the Army?"

"I'm going to open a restaurant," he said proudly. "I been cooking all my life and I'm good at it. Been all over the world. Been to Germany and France. Me and my buddies drove to Hawai'i. But I found out that there ain't no place like Wilson. I'm going to start my restaurant right here. Gonna call it *The Pig and Fowl*."

"That's a very good name. So, you are going to focus on fried chicken and barbeque?"

"Yep."

They arrived at Viola Street much too quickly. Wiley said, "I'll be back in a couple of months. I'd like to come see you again."

And she said, "Okay."

He squeezed her hand tightly and left her on her front porch, just before dark, and just before her curfew of seven o'clock.

•

Wiley returned in June of 1944. At first, he didn't tell Beulah his secret and the reason he was in plain clothes. It wouldn't have mattered anyway; they were both in love. She heard the toot of his horn and she ran to the front porch to greet him. Seeing her made him bring the bike to a screeching halt, and she ran into his arms and wrapped her legs around his back. They did not kiss; that would have been inappropriate, but she placed a finger over her lips to quiet him and she hopped on the back of his bike.

He wanted her to meet someone, he told her, and they took the long ride uptown and through Daniel Hill before they arrived at Wiggins Street. Beulah had never seen that part of town. She was surprised that it even existed, being so close to the white settlement. Wiley parked his bike and held her hand as they walked up the steps to his mother's house.

Easter was frying fish.

Wiley said, "Beulah, this is my mother. Mama, this is Beulah. Ain't she pretty?"

Easter wiped her hands on her apron. "Yeah, she look all right." She eyed the girl up and down. "Y'all hungry?"

"No, ma'am. Thank you." Beulah felt a little uncomfortable with Wiley's mother staring at her like that, but it was her home training that made her decline a meal she really wanted; fried fish was her favorite meal. But she had been taught that it was impolite to accept a meal away from home. She wanted to make a good impression and eating at Easter's house on her first visit was not the way to do it.

"Well, y'all make yourselves at home."

The house was full of people who were drinking and playing cards. Wiley led Beulah to a back room where they could talk in private. She followed him eagerly—anything to get away from the scornful look of his mother. He offered her a seat on the bed, the only furniture in that room, and then he sat down next to her. He kissed her and felt her stiffen.

"What's the matter?" He was genuinely concerned, she could tell.

"I don't know. So many people out there."

"Relax. They won't come in here."

He kissed her again, and this time he felt her loosen up a bit. He unbuttoned her blouse and fondled her breasts. She returned his kisses with enthusiasm. They were both nervous, but they each had anticipated this moment for a long time. She let him guide her, convinced that it was the right thing to do and the right time to do it. She was already seventeen. Some of her friends and all of her sisters were married already. They shared stories with Beulah about the time they spent with their husbands.

Now, Beulah was curious at the very least, and hopeful that Wiley would make her dreams come true. He adored her. The scent of her hair, her skin. Vanilla. He was ever so gentle, but she was as innocent as the first hint of sunrise. Her body trembled as she anticipated him. When he possessed her, she cried out in pain. Nobody had warned her about that. The tears rolled from her eyes and moistened the pillow. Wiley kissed them away. He knew at that moment that she was his and his alone, and before long, Beulah had discovered a truth she could not share with anyone.

They saw each other every day after that. It was summer, and Beulah, pretending to look for work, would get up and leave the house every morning. They met at Langley's Grocery on Reid Street, and they rode to Easter's house every time. On one of these visits, toward the end of July, Wiley told Beulah his secret.

"I'm not in the Army anymore," he said. "I didn't like it

because I was too far away from you. So, I quit. I learned a lot while I was there, though. They taught me how to say 'Sir,' instead of 'Suh,' so I figure the experience was worth it."

He did not understand the look on her face. Couldn't read her mind. He tilted his head a little to look at her. "What are you thinking? Are you disappointed?"

"Not at all," she said. "I have some news, too."

"Really? What?"

She looked at the ground. "I'm going to have a baby."

"Well, well, well!" he said. "I guess you gonna have to marry me then."

She stuck out her tongue. "And I guess you're going to need a job."

•

They decided to wait a while before telling their folks. Her father would be devastated, and Wiley would need to secure that job to convince the old man that things would be okay for them. He went back to the Do Drop Inn where Charlie offered him part-time work.

Wiley was amazed that the same group of patrons were still there. One of the men, Doug Thompson, had once told him, "If you ever want to make some real money, call me." So, when Wiley saw him enter the restaurant one day, he greeted him cheerfully.

"How you doing Mr. Thompson?"

"I'm doing fine, Wiley. Glad to see you back. How have you been?"

"Can't complain. I was wondering if that offer still stands?"

"Yep. Just let me know when you're ready."

"Oh, I'm ready right now, Sir."

"It's hard work. You up for that?"

"Yes, Sir."

"Okay. Well turn in your apron and meet me at my truck. I'll clear it with Charlie."

Wiley did exactly as he was told.

Doug Thompson's business was dry wall plastering.

He took Wiley on as an apprentice and taught him everything he knew. He admired the way the young man learned quickly. Wiley was first on the job in the mornings and last to leave. He made no excuses, and he worked hard and independently. He soon became an assistant to the foreman of the crew. Wiley was young, strong and innovative, and he invented ways to make his work his own—rosettes and 'icicles' hung from the ceilings; plastered floral designs were on the walls. It was his signature. A wall was a canvas to him and plaster became his art. In a few short weeks he had earned enough money to ask Solomon Sherrod for his daughter's hand in marriage. It never occurred to him that the answer might be *no*.

So, when Wiley and Beulah approached her father one Sunday afternoon in September, they both wore smiles of confidence.

"Mr. Sherrod, Sir, my name is Wiley Williams, and I am here to ask for your daughter's hand."

The old man sat reading with his pipe in the right corner of his mouth. He did not look up. "Which one?" It was a moot question, full of annoyance and contempt. All his other daughters were married.

"Ah...Beulah, Sir."

Wiley had dressed for the occasion in his grey suit. He held his hat in his left hand and extended the other to Solomon Sherrod. Beulah fumbled with the cuff of her sleeve. Her father peered over his glasses, puffed on his pipe and then appeared to go back to his reading. "She's too young," he said.

"Papa, I'm seventeen," Beulah whined.

"That's too young for you to be thinking about getting married, girl. You still have another year of schooling."

Beulah and Wiley looked at each other. The old man cleared his throat. "I said 'No.' Why are you still here?"

"Um..." Wiley started. "She's, um, pregnant, Sir."

Beulah's father put down his book and removed his pipe slowly. He gazed accusingly at his daughter. "That true?"

"Yes, Sir." She could see the hurt in his eyes. He stood up.

"I thought you wanted better than that. Hard as I work to give you a better life. This is the way you repay me? I thought you wanted to be a teacher. How could you stoop so low? Shame on you, girl!"

Beulah regarded that comment as an attack on her virtue. He was judging her. Condemning her. She fought back in the only way she could. "You didn't do so good when you got Booker T."

Booker T. was the child the old man made with a woman other than Josephine, his wife. Because the woman was young and incapable of raising him, Solomon brought him home and Josephine raised him as her own. They had four children at the time, had lost two or three, and even though she was hurt, Josephine gave Booker T. the love and nurturing that she gave her own children.

Beulah's statement took the breath right out of Solomon Sherrod. It was an indictment. An invasion of his privacy, and a reminder that he, himself, was not perfect. To think that it was uttered by his favorite child cut him to the quick, and it hurt him badly. He staggered backwards and sank in his chair. In a moment he seemed to age a dozen years. He never spoke to her again.

Wiley and Beulah took a bus to Dillon, South Carolina. Named for John W. Dillon who helped orchestrate the railroad through that area, the town sat right in the middle between "Fort Bragg, North Carolina and Jackson, South Carolina. At the time it was called The Wedding Capital of the East. People as young as fourteen could get married there for three dollars. Soldiers about to deploy overseas, or anyone else who needed to marry quickly, found themselves lining up for a small wedding ceremony.

It was cool that morning, so Beulah wore her navy-blue wool dress. By the time they reached Charlotte, however, she started to feel very warm. She convinced herself that she was just nervous as all new brides tend to be. Marriage had not been a part of her immediate plans, but with a baby on the way, there was little else to do. When the bus pulled into the hot and unusually humid station at Dillon, she had already opened her collar, and she dabbed at the sweat on her neck. The temperature was close to a hundred degrees, and the air was still. Wiley took off his jacket and held it across his shoulder with an index finger.

It was so hot in that little town. An Indian summer. *Pneumonia weather* Beulah called it. They walked to the courthouse and Beulah filled out some papers for their wedding. He had bought her a ring, a simple gold band, and he bought her some red earbobs as a wedding present.

She was in her world. This beautiful man wanted her enough to defy her father. She was going to have his baby. Nothing could be more perfect.

The magistrate's wife served as a witness and Wiley and Beulah were married at four o'clock in the afternoon of September 16, 1944. Afterwards, they bought fried chicken at a local spot, and they sat on the curb to eat it. They had to wait until the next day to return to Wilson and, since there were no hotels for coloreds at that time, they slept on the bench outside the bus station.

The ride home was a difficult one. It had begun to rain, and the wind rocked the bus with such force that the driver had to struggle to control it. In their eagerness to have and to hold, neither of them had checked the weather report or *Poor Richard's Almanac*, which Beulah's mother, Josephine, relied on as heavily as she did the Bible. So, by the time they reached the North Carolina border on the return trip, the Great Atlantic Hurricane was in full force. It was a tropical cyclone that would usher in a long, wet winter of destructive hurricanes, tornadoes, hail and straight-line winds and floods.

When they reached Wilson, the water was ankle deep. They held each other closely as they walked to Darden Alley. The winds threatened to blow them away, and the rain was hard as bullets. Trash stirred from the ground, trees broke, and the gloomy sky was the color of a battleship.

Dolly Mae, Wiley's cousin, had agreed to let them stay with her and her family. When the newly married couple arrived, they were tired, wet and hungry. Dolly Mae served them neckbones and rice, black-eyed peas, and cabbage, and they settled into what would turn into a three-year long stay.

They both believed they would live the "happiness ever after" kind of life they had heard about in the fairy tales. But the Great Atlantic Hurricane, the physical storm, seemingly predicted the metaphorical storm that was to be their marriage. The Great Atlantic killed 390 people along the east coast, including Doug Thompson. It sank war ships and caused over 100 million dollars in damages. It was the predecessor of a variety of horrible storms that winter. In October, hurricanes raged through the Carolinas, destroying homes, buildings and crops. November brought over fifty inches of rain. The drywall business was put on hold for the entire winter and Wiley could not work.

He took to gambling. He was good at it. Most of the time he could turn two dollars into fifty in a single night, but it took *all* night. Beulah got accustomed to sleeping alone.

She could not cook, so he had to teach her. She had little experience in keeping a house clean, so he taught her that, too. She followed his instructions to the letter and, regardless of the time he returned home, she'd get up and fix him something to eat. They were deliriously happy, Wiley and Beulah. He knew his job was to provide for his family. She knew her role, her place. She didn't ask for much. Though he came into her life riding a red bicycle rather than a big white horse, he was her prince, nonetheless. She was satisfied to belong to him.

Fifteen

Easter never believed in fairy tales or nursery rhymes.
She was a very practical woman who did not subscribe to
the moral mandates of those stories. She had rejected
the only direction her mother had tried to give her, and
she had created herself by living life according to what
felt right to her. She did, however, believe in the physical
superiority of men. They were made that way on purpose.
They had to fight off the enemy, do the hard work, put the
garbage on the street on collection day, and protect their
women.

Dave Evans could do all those things and then some.
Before they met, Easter had a short list of men who
were not members of her regular clientele. She would
occasionally allow one of them to share her bed, but it
was for maintenance purposes only. She surrendered
no emotion, no commitment, and the next day he was
just another experience. Dave, however, was the whole
package. He fought for her, fulfilled her emotional needs.
He was the best lover she had ever known. He worked
hard all day long and when he knocked off at noon on
Saturdays, he brought his pay home to her. He even
convinced the cops that twenty-five percent was nothing
less than extortion, and they agreed to reduce their take
to ten percent.

But Easter never let Dave know his value in her life. She was determined to keep him on edge, keep him wondering when she would tire of him and find someone else. Nobody ever knew where he came from. He had no family, no past, no history. He just showed up at her house that Sunday morning and they started living together. Until he was willing to fully share himself, she had to protect herself by being as mysterious as he was.

Of course, she had questions that generally arose in the course of their conversations, but he had a way about him that allowed him to evade them beautifully. He'd flash her a gleaming smile or slap her on the butt. Sometimes he'd change the subject by asking her a question of his own, and she would find herself immersed in what she perceived to be his genuine interest in her family. He listened intently and never judged her.

She felt safe with him. She loved the way his fingers ravaged her hair when they made love. He said it felt like corn silk, and he made her promise to never cut it.

Because of Easter's business they rarely had the opportunity to go anywhere. But on the day that she blew a hole in the ceiling, she agreed to take Sundays off so they could spend some time together. Easter hired her favorite customer as her assistant so she would not lose revenue. She and Dave committed to celebrating special occasions—her birthday, Easter Sunday, Christmas, and Valentine's Day. Once in a while they would go to a movie. Sometimes they rode up to Raleigh, taking the back roads and remarking on the farmlands and the animals. The ride through the country was refreshing with the scent of freshly plowed earth and fertilizer. It reminded Easter of her roots and showed her how far she had come. But most of the time, they just went to the juke joint, and she danced the night away. She was almost fifteen years older than Dave and, while the numbers did not bother either of them, Dave was soon to learn that Easter was very possessive and very jealous. She was also very strong.

So, on one of these excursions to the dance hall,

when Dave finished playing and singing a few down-home blues songs, a snappy young thing made her way to him and rubbed his thigh.

She taunted Easter directly. Dave tried to push her back, but the woman insisted on getting close to him.

"I wouldn't do that if I were you," Easter said to her.

"What you gon' do, old lady?"

Surprisingly, Easter stayed calm. She took a sip of her drink and put the glass on the bar. She glared at the woman, but she folded her arms and said nothing.

Seeing this, Dave put his arm around Easter. "C'mon baby, let's go." He smiled politely at the woman.

"Uh huh! Just what I thought," the woman said, and she grabbed Dave's arm. "Let's go dance, sweetheart," she said.

Easter snatched a plank of wood off the wall. The nails stubbornly clung to the wood, and Easter proceeded to beat the woman senseless with it. With every blow there was a different squirt of blood. The screams of the woman started a riot and Dave had to fight all the men in the joint. The piano man kept on playing and the whole scene looked like a choreographed production. Finally, after ducking knives and broken bottles, he managed to get Easter out of the place, and they ran all the way home.

But Dave was not happy with Easter's behavior. The house was full of people, and they went into the house shouting at each other.

"You were wrong!" he told her.

"*Whaddya* mean I was wrong? She called me *old.* And she put her hands on you!"

"That ain't got shit to do with nothing! Am I yo' man? Am I yo' man?!"

"Yeah, you my man. That's what I'm talking about! She disrespected me. *And* you!"

"Well, if I'm yo' man, why can't you just trust me? Can't nobody make me do nothing I don't want to do."

A man stood and looked like he was trying to get between them. Easter raised a finger and said, "You…

stay out of this. Don't you *ever* interfere with me and my man." She turned back to Dave. Her left hand was on her hip; her right hand waved a finger in his face as she advanced towards him. "Oh. So, it's okay for women to feel you up right in front of me? How'd you like it if I let a man touch me in public? Huh? How'd you like it if I was grinning like a Cheshire cat at him? How'd you like it—"

In a flash he saw his mother, loud, drunken, abusive and accusing. He slapped Easter with all his might. She went reeling across the room and, sliding into the leg of the couch, her face bumped against it. As she staggered to her feet, she shook her head and wiped the blood from her lip. In a moment she was composed. The people in the room stared at Dave incredulously, and they frantically searched for an escape route. They all knew her, and they expected that a big fight was coming. But Dave and Easter were positioned in such a way that the door was blocked. So, they waited for her to react. Nobody moved. In that moment, pregnant with anticipation, Easter shook her head again as if to regain her sense. She did not fight him back, even though she could. She did not call the police, either, as some women tend to do. She excused herself and went into the kitchen to make herself a drink.

Dave felt stupid, awkward. He expected her to throw something or put him out. Yes, that at least. But when she seemed to have no reaction to the slap, she confused him.In bed that night he apologized for hitting her.

"Uh uh. Don't do that. You sonofabitch. If you can hit me in front of everybody you should apologize in front of everybody."

"I'm really sorry. I don't know what happened. You came at me with your hand on your hip, like you were my mama, and everything went black. I'm so sorry."

"No matter. You were right. I was wrong. It's good to know that you care enough to correct me. Go to sleep and forget about it."

With that line she was as honest as she had ever been, but it frightened Dave. He knew her story and her temper. He knew because she had told him. He could not sleep. He stayed awake most of the night watching her. And when Easter uttered a groan of oblivion and took deep, rhythmic breaths, he slipped quietly out of bed and left her house.

Easter awoke to the first real disappointment of her life. She had told the truth, but Dave left anyway. Now, she was alone again, but the bitter truth was that Dave had become her anchor. He was the light of her life, and she was willing to do anything to please him. She sent messages to him by other workers at the quarry, asking him to come on home, but they reported that he only smiled when he received them.

She was confused and angry. How could he just walk away like that? She had allowed him to mark his territory by branding her with a black eye and split lip in front of everybody. Still, he left when there was no doubt that she belonged to him. She belonged *with* him. She thought they were made for each other and now...well, now...she had to devise a plan to live without him.

It was her business that made that part difficult. Dave had served as her protection, a bouncer of sorts whenever a drunken customer got unruly. He even helped out around the house. He worked all day, came home and took a bath, and then he emptied ash trays and took out the rubbish. She loved that part of him. He had given her many glorious months of bliss, and she realized that she had become dependent on him because of it.

But then, quick as summer lightning, she switched her mindset. She had survived the first forty-one years of her life without him; she could survive now. The only difference was that Easter was not as vibrant as she used to be. The welcoming chorus of "Hey baby" and "Come on in, sweetheart," changed to "How much time do you need?" and "How much do you plan to spend?"

Her clients knew it was because she was grieving the loss of Dave and, after a while, they managed to convince him to talk with her. He did, and when she tried to coax him to come home, he said, "I can't do that."

"Why not?"

"'Cause I start the night shift in a couple of months. The boss hired me to guard the grounds. That means I have to sleep during the day."

"What's that got to do with you coming home?"

"I can't sleep with all these people in here."

"Oh."

Neither of them said anything more for a few minutes, as if they were both trying to discover a solution to the problem. Then Dave said, "You know...I really do make enough money to take care of us. You have money stashed everywhere, coffee cans, shoe boxes, even stuffed between the mattress and the box spring. You could retire. You don't have to keep doing this."

"You want me to give up my business? Are you crazy?"

"No. Listen. You been doing this for a long time. With all that money you got stored away, we could have a good life on what I make."

Easter folded her arms and said nothing. Dave realized that he was not getting anywhere with her, so he turned to leave.

"Where are you going?" She asked him. "We haven't finished this conversation."

"I'm going back to where I been ever since I left you. I'm telling you, girl. If you want me, you got to give this up. That's the only way I'm coming back here."

She thought about it for just a moment. Indeed, she loved him, needed him to be close. She had tried to let a man take care of her once and it did not work. But Dave was right. She had enough money saved to last for the rest of her life if she was careful and spent wisely. Her house was paid for. All she really had to worry about was taxes, insurance, utilities and food. She would not have to be dependent on him in case he tried to dominate her the way some men do when their wives don't work.

"How long did you say before you start the night

shift?"

"Two months."

"Then I'll do it."

They embraced and his touch was unusually tender. He caressed her face, and eventually they made love. As they lay in the aftermath, he said to her, "I am so sorry I hit you. I didn't even mean to do it. Everything just went black. The way you pointed your finger at me with your hand on your hip like that reminded me of my mama. I felt a rush of heat all over, and I couldn't see anything. Just blackness."

"Tell me about her."

"Not much to tell really."

"There must be something to make you mad enough to leave me."

"I wasn't mad at you. I was mad at *her.*"

"Then why did you leave me?"

"'Cause I had to. I looked at your face all fucked up and I realized that I had done it. I couldn't stand to see you that way. 'Specially since it was my mama I really wanted to hit."

"Well, I don't know much about church business, but I do believe it is a sin to hit your mother. Guess I was just convenient, huh? What did she do to make you so angry now?"

He rose and paced the floor. It seemed like he went into some kind of trance as he remembered his childhood.

She used to beat me all the time. All the time. She would get drunk early in the morning and then she'd lie around all day barking orders at me. David, do this. David, do that. Fix me a drink. Bring me a cigarette. Take care of your little brother, David. Be a good boy, David. I had to light the cigarettes myself. And if I didn't put enough whiskey in her drink, or enough mustard on her ham sandwich, she'd beat me with whatever was available, the hairbrush, the fire poke, a belt.

My daddy left right before my little brother was born. I was five. Look like she wanted to punish him for leaving, so she took it out on me. I couldn't do nothing right to satisfy her. Hard as I tried. She would stand over me with her hand on her hip and point her finger in my face. Just like you did. And after she finished yelling at me and cussing me out, she would grab something and beat the shit out of me.

Then one day when I was eight and my brother was three, we went into the woods to find huckleberries. We spent most of the day having fun, you know? On the way back, I put him on my shoulders 'cause it was getting dark and he walked too slow. Mama would beat me for sure if I was out past dark. I started running with him and the bucket. Him and the bucket. Oooooh!

He placed both hands on the wall and hung his head. Easter went to him and rubbed his back. When he turned to face her, she saw that his eyes were as red as coal fire.

It was an accident. I swear. I didn't mean it. I-I didn't mean it! I tripped over a log and he went tumbling forward. He hit his head on a rock and—he—died. He just died right there. I picked him up and took him home. His neck was broke. My mama acted like I had done it on purpose. She screamed and begged Jesus to take it back. And then she started to beat on me with a fury I never knew she had. She beat me so bad that day, I almost died myself. So, my grandma took me away from her and she kept me until she died. I was fifteen. I been on my own ever since.

His body shook with sobs. Easter held him in her arms. "I don't know what to say," she told him. "I wish I had been there to make it all better."

"I thought I was over it," he said. "I don't ever want to go there again. I don't want to hurt you just because I'm still pissed off at her."

"What was her name?"

"Mama is all I ever knew. I was so young, and after my grandma took me, I never saw my mama again. Never saw my daddy after he left, either. My grandma's name was Betsy. I know that much. That's why I never told you anything about my past. I don't know much about it myself."

"Thank you for trusting me enough to tell me. Do you

feel better now that you have shared with me?"

"No. I had kept that secret for so long. Nobody knew, and I pushed it way down deep so nobody *would* know. Now you have brought it to the surface, and I have to think about it. I don't want to think about it. It hurts. And I don't want you to be caught up in the middle of it ever again."

"I'll try to be careful. I don't want to get hit like that again, either."

He smiled and wiped his nose. "Okay."

She was determined to be true to the promise to be careful because she was only willing to take that one slap. She would also be true to the promise of closing her business. It would take a while for folks to get used to the way Easter met them at the door and turned them away. For the next few weeks, she continued to provide for some of her favorites, but they had to be gone by four in the afternoon. On the day that she finally realized that pretending to be unemployed was more than she could handle, her clients came to know the real Easter.

It was almost time for Dave to come home, and she had to clean the house and make his dinner. She told them all to get out. When nothing happened, she went through the house kicking open doors and yelling obscenities. "I want all you motherfuckers out of my house right now!"

One of the men crossed his legs. "You just a spitfire hellraiser, ain't you?"

Easter went to her room and came back with her shotgun. The house cleared out in less than a minute.

Sixteen

Wiley and Beulah continued to live with Dolly Mae and her family in the big house on Darden Alley. Their first child was born in March of 1945. Work was still slow for Wiley, but gambling was often productive enough for them to eat and share a little with Dolly Mae. The arrangement worked well for a long time and then, When Beulah's oldest sister, Aileen, divorced her husband and moved to Durham, her house on Queen Street became available. Wiley and Beulah quickly rented it and moved in.

It was a three-room in-way house. It had a front porch with a swing, a back porch with a spigot, two bedrooms and a small kitchen. The toilet was in the backyard. The land was narrow, but deep. Perfect for a garden.

Beulah was overjoyed to have her own place. She set up housekeeping with great enthusiasm, making sure she had all the finest things: sheets, towels, silverware. She and her daughter, Barbara Ann, spent many evenings reading, coloring, playing games and listening to the radio. The Uncle Remus stories, Mr. and Mrs. North, and The Shadow Knows kept them occupied when Wiley was not at home.

She was grateful that her child was born healthy; grateful that Barbara Ann learned things quickly. Beulah taught the child to read early, and by three Barbara Ann could say The Lord's Prayer in French, and she could read all the Dick and Jane stories.

Beulah was happy with her little family. Barbara Ann was good company, almost like a toy. Beulah kept the child dressed up like a doll—flouncy dresses with stiffly starched pinafores and shiny, patent leather T-straps. As the girl grew, they played hopscotch and jacks and jump rope together.

Still, something was missing. She could not define it, but an emptiness was always there hovering over her. She thought at first that it was the abbreviation of her education and her desire to travel. She secretly wished she had waited to have a child when she was about twenty-five instead of eighteen. She wanted a house on Green Street, a house that had a little white picket fence and steps that led from the sidewalk to her home. Green Street represented success, and if she had gone to college, she would have been able to purchase a home there.

Then she thought that the void in her life was the severed relationship between her and her father. She decided to make amends. Even if he had not been able to forgive her, surely, he could not resist his charming little granddaughter.

She went to visit her parents' home. Her mother met her at the door and motioned for her to sit on the front porch.

Josephine Sherrod sat next to her daughter on the tin swing. She brought Barbara Ann to her lap, and after a few hugs and compliments, she sat the child down on the edge of the porch. She sat wringing her hands and Beulah perceived her to be extremely nervous.

"Where's Papa?" Beulah asked.

"He's in the parlor."

"What's he doing?"

"Reading."

"Does he know I'm here?"

"Yes. He knows."

"Well, I came to see him."

"Leave it alone, child."

"Mama, I just came to tell him that I'm sorry. I didn't mean to hurt him so badly."

"I'm sure he knows that."

"How's he doing?"

"He's been feeling a might poorly lately."

Beulah stood up. "I'm going in to see him."

Her mother grabbed her wrist. "Uh uh. Don't do that. Like I said, you leave it alone. You hear?"

Realizing that her father was still mad at her, Beulah went back home. But she carried a burden of guilt for which she could not help blaming on Barbara Ann. She loved her child, but the thought that Barbara Ann was the cause and the object of contention between her and her father crept into her consciousness every time she looked at the little girl. It was a wound that would never heal, a hardness that would never soften.

Solomon Sherrod died in February of 1948. He had been born Solomon Sherrard, but Elmer, his youngest son, changed the spelling of the name when he was in school. It became official when he joined the Army. The story goes that Elmer was only fifteen years old at the time. He altered his birth certificate to show that he was sixteen, and the new spelling of the name covered for his lie. The family members liked that spelling, so they all adopted it.

Later that same year, on November 24, Beulah had another child, a boy. They named him Wiley, Jr., as almost all families did for their firstborn sons. His birth was marked with trouble from the start. For one thing, Wiley was not present when Jr. was born. He had told Beulah that he was going to the World Series in New York. They had argued about him leaving when she was so close to her time. He slapped her and insisted that the tickets had already been purchased. He was determined to go. Beulah took the slap as a part of marriage—nothing really important. He didn't mean to hurt her, of course. He just meant to show her the correct way to be a good wife.

She should be happy. She had everything a woman could possibly want: a lovely home, a beautiful child and one on the way, and the most handsome husband in town.

With her investigative spirit, Beulah went to the library and searched the encyclopedia. She learned that the World Series always happens in October, and in 1948 it was held in Cleveland, Ohio. The Cleveland Indians won. Through her clandestine inquiries, she found out that Wiley had no Veteran benefits. He had never been to Germany or France. In fact, he only stayed in the Army for two months, discharged because they found out that he could not read or write. She sat reading the encyclopedia one day when she discovered that Hawai'i was an island. Nobody can just drive there. Now, she recognized her own vulnerability, her gullibility to believe anything Wiley told her, and she now knew that he was a braggart and a liar. She was suspicious of every single thing he ever said to her after that.

For another thing, Wiley Jr. was dark-skinned. Since Beulah, Wiley and Barbara Ann were all paper bag tan, Big Wiley could not see how that was possible. He suspected her of being with someone else. He did not accuse her directly; his plan was to wait until she brought up the subject.

They were in bed one night when the conversation about color came up. They started off by talking about money.

"We are going to be all right," Wiley said. "I'm sure work will pick up. Look at all the construction that's going on around here. I promised to take good care of you. I love you. I always did."

"Well, if you love me so much why didn't you use protection to keep me from getting big? I was only seventeen."

The gate was open wide. This was his time to walk through it and get some answers. He said, "I'm not so sure I bigged you."

She looked at him with disbelief. "Lord, Wiley. You

ought to be ashamed of yourself. Barbr'ann looks just like you."

"But Junior don't. I don't know where he came from."

In the fall of the following year, Wiley was at a poker game when one of the men accused him of cheating. He had a royal flush in spades, but the accuser had an ace of spades in his hand. All eyes were on him as the men reached into their pockets or their socks for weapons. Wiley, unarmed, put his hand inside his jacket and stood up. This gave him an advantage.

"Don't move," he said. "Now I am going to back away from here and y'all just stay calm. That way nobody will get hurt. I ain't got no need to cheat. Got everything I want."

One of the men shouted, "Nigger, what you got?"

"Well, I got this winning hand, and I got this money." He scooped up the cash with his left hand. "I got me a car, a good woman, and two kids at home."

"You ain't got shit," the man said. "You living in someone else's house. You strut around here like you the king of the land, and that wife of yours running over on Hines Street every chance she gets."

If he had been able to read Wiley would have known the truth about Beulah's visits across town, and he might have been able to squash the rumors about her. There had been an article in The Confidential, a neighborhood newspaper that focused on gossip, and it told the story of Beulah's visits to her sister three times a week. But he couldn't read, so he saw the man's comments as a revelation. It shocked Wiley, especially since all the other men agreed. They knew something he didn't. It also made him think about Junior and how black he was. The muscles in Wiley's face twitched as he mumbled, "What the hell you talkin' 'bout?"

"Oh, you don't have to take my word for it. Just be on the corner of Hines and Pender streets tomorrow 'bout one o'clock. See for yourself."

The men laughed then, and Wiley was in a huff. It

couldn't be true. Of course, it couldn't be true. He knew how to handle his woman. She was always at home when he got there no matter what time of day or night.

But he had no trust in women. None whatsoever. His own mother had abandoned him when he was a child. Too often he had observed the dutiful, hard working men drop their waitress wives off at the front of Do Drop Inn, but before the day was through the women would go into Charlie's office and close the door. More than half of the women in his mother's whorehouse were married, and he envisioned all kinds of things that could happen if their husbands ever found out how they spent their days.

It never occurred to him that his own wife would fit into that category of trampy, loose women. He had given her a good life. He gave her money that she shared with her family. So what if he slapped her around a little bit? She needed to pay attention to what he tried to teach her. She had to understand that it was all a part of keeping her secure.

No. It couldn't possibly be true. They must have her confused with someone else. But the men at the poker game had laughed at him, humiliated him. He didn't want people talking about his wife that way, so he would be at Pender and Hines tomorrow and put all that nonsense to rest.

The next day Wiley dressed in his work clothes and told Beulah that he had an emergency job to do. He would be gone all day. He wanted chicken pastry and cornbread for dinner. He left some money on the mantle.

●

She was restless. So much had happened in such a short time. Five years ago, she was single, carefree, and planning her life to be so different from what it had turned out to be. She had had choices of other suitors, but she chose Wiley. Now, at twenty-two, she felt unfulfilled, empty. It took exactly one hour to clean her house and put her children out to play. All her siblings had God-given talents that they could use to keep themselves busy.

Flora had her sewing; Doretta had her garden. Minnie Bell was a gifted cook, and Shird, with only a third-grade education, built houses by himself. But Beulah's only gift, as she saw it, was her intellect, and since she married, she had not had much opportunity to use it. She had no books to read, no hobbies, and only one friend, Louise, a neighbor who worked in service all day and was, therefore, unavailable to help Beulah get through her day. She needed a project, something she could do with her hands to keep her occupied. With him gone all day and sometimes well into the night, she felt uninspired, unmotivated.

By now, Flora had three children, and she was pregnant again. It took her five years to have one child and then she had a baby every year. She lived on Suggs Street near Elvie Street School. She took in sewing to help make ends meet, and she offered to teach Beulah how to sew.

Beulah hired a sixteen-year-old girl to watch her children from eleven to four almost every day. On most of those days, she made the trek to Flora's house for sewing lessons. Sometimes they would work on a project together. Being left-handed, she had difficulty negotiating the scissors, but she managed to cut patterns slowly and hem the dresses. Other times she and Flora would enjoy lemonade or iced tea and just sit and talk. It was stimulating, adult conversation, and Beulah soon became addicted to her routine of walking over to her sister's house and sharing her company.

It was a long way from Queen Street. Beulah set out at about eleven in the morning. She walked straight down Reid Street to Nash and turned right. At the corner of Vick, she stopped to exchange cordial greetings with an old classmate from high school that she had not seen in a while, and then she resumed her walk. It was a beautiful day. Seventy-two degrees and the sun shone brightly. She wished she had brought an umbrella to shield her from the sun. She reached Pender and decided to cross to the shady side of the street before she turned left. As she waited for the traffic light, it started to rain. Without warning, the clear, blue sky opened up and emptied its bladder. The sun was still shining. The devil must be beating his wife, she thought. That's the story her mother had told her when Beulah questioned such an unusual circumstance. The rain only lasted for a few seconds, but she was soaked clean through. She bent down and lifted the tail end of her skirt to wipe her face, and when she stood up again, Wiley was standing there.

"Where are you going?" he asked through clenched teeth.

"What are you doing here? I thought you had to work."

"I asked you a question. Where the fuck are you going?"

"I'm going to Flora's house."

"Right. Flora. She cloaking for you and that college boy?"

"What? No! I'm not doing anything."

"Get in the car."

He grabbed her arm, and she pulled away from him. He picked her up at the waist. "I said, get your ass in this car."

That was the day that sealed her fate. He took her to the woods that night, tied her to a tree, and pointed a shotgun towards her face. He held her hostage all night long. He could not believe she would do this to him. He was Hollywood handsome. He was Wiley Williams. He deserved better, and he could not let her get away with it.

Seventeen

Beulah believed that it was the strength of God almighty that brought her out of the woods alive that night. She had prayed hard, and even though she knew that she had not betrayed her marriage, she also knew that Wiley was capable of killing. He had told her about the man in the country. So, she prayed, and when Wiley finally put the shotgun back in the trunk of his car and took her home, she made a promise to God that she would stay with him and take care of him for the rest of their lives.

It was a promise she would keep for another sixty years. Regardless of what he did to her, she kept that promise. He beat her, and she took it. He gambled away the money; she got a job. He left her and made babies with another woman, but she maintained a home ready to receive him whenever he returned.

She saw it as a natural thing. It was her punishment for defying her father. She told herself that man is not monogamous. All men cheat and lie; hers was no different. But, she felt safe in the fact that she was still married to him, and she believed in her heart that he would never, ever change that. For the next few years, he would come into her life as easily as the shift of the wind, and just as easily he would leave again.

She started to notice a pattern with him, though. As

they continued their life together, it became increasingly violent. In private they were all lovey-dovey. In public, however, he was downright cruel. It seemed to be important to him to let everyone know when he beat her. The beatings were always sporadic, without warning and, seemingly, without provocation. One minute he'd call her "Honey," and the next minute he'd call her a jinky-assed witch. She took the liberty one time and returned his insult. "You are a crazy sonofabitch!" He chased her through the house, wrestled her to the floor, and choked her until she passed out. Then he picked her up, sprinkled water on her face and said, "Come on, baby. Come on out of it."

On several occasions Beulah ran to a neighbor's house and called the police. They arrested him and kept him in jail for the weekend. By Monday morning, however, she missed him and felt sorry for him. So, she went uptown to take up the warrant. The police were very skeptical about answering calls of domestic violence in black families. In many cases they had gone to a house where violence had been reported. Many of those times it was a man beating up on a woman, and when they arrived, the woman would jump on them if and when they tried to lock up the man. There were few laws governing domestic violence at the time, so the police took the stance that if they did not see anything happen, the best they could do was make one of the parties leave for a while to cool off. Within hours they would return to the house, and most often than not, they found the couple hugging and kissing.

One time Wiley beat Beulah so badly that she actually did leave him. She took her children to Durham to live with Aileen. Wiley was intimidated by Aileen. She was nineteen years older than Beulah, and she did not play when it came to her baby sister. Truth be told, Wiley was indeed scared shitless of Minnie Bell, too. Minnie Bell was tough, hard core, and she fought like a man. She had the scars to prove it. So he usually stayed away when Beulah found asylum at either of their houses.

Aileen lived on Dover Street. The house was flat on the ground and Aileen kept cedar mulch around it. The street had a huge hill and Aileen's house was at the bottom. Thinking that the separation was going to be permanent, Beulah enrolled Barbara Ann in school at Lyon Park Elementary where the child was sent to first grade.

Aileen's house was always clean, especially the bathroom. A bottle of Listerine sat on the counter, and a large gallon-sized jar was on the floor. It held loose cigarettes, Lucky Strike. Her husband, Henry Randall, was now retired from the Navy and he worked at Liggett & Myers Tobacco company. He was obviously a good provider; they had a Duncan Fife sofa in the living room.

Beulah maintained that Barbara Ann was fancy, "just like Aileen," and she frequently compared herself to her oldest sister. In this comparison, she saw herself as weak and submissive. Aileen was strong and domineering. Wiley could shut Beulah up with a simple look; Aileen never let Henry into any conversation. Every time he tried to say something, she'd tell him, "Now hush a minute, Henry. Hush a minute. There was a smugness about her that most folks did not understand. She'd raise a shoulder and tilt her head towards the wall when she explained that the little tin on her mantle contained "Chocolate covered ants imported from Germany."

A part of Aileen needed to have nice, expensive things. She worked hard in a sewing factory. She furnished her house with mahogany and cherrywood. She wore nice clothes and shoes. A mink stole wrapped her shoulders on Sundays.

Henry generally just talked to the children because they were the only ones willing to give him audience. He told them travel stories. His favorite was his encounter with a little boy in Germany who had impressed Henry with his speech. The way he exaggerated the kid's pronouncement of "chocolate" made the children squeal with laughter: "I had a *chock-o-lit* bar one time." It made Henry feel important to entertain the children.

In her sister's eyes Beulah could not do anything right. Beulah made the beds; Aileen did them over. She washed dishes, but she did not rinse or dry them. Aileen had a fit about that. Aileen liked swordfish and spinach; Beulah liked fried chicken and collards. With all this in mind and the coldness of that winter, Beulah acknowledged a desire to return to her husband. The sleet storm that year was horrendous, and she watched the chains on the tires of cars as they struggled, slipping and sliding up the steep hill when their occupants tried to get to work. The school bus gave up and did not take the children to school that day; it stayed parked in front of Aileen's house until the ice melted.

Spring eventually came and Beulah started going to Wilson every day. She took Barbara Ann with her; Henry watched Wiley, Jr. They boarded the bus early in the morning after breakfast. Barbara Ann sat on her mother's lap and together they counted in French the rows of corn or tobacco, or whatever as they whizzed past them on the hot, bumpy ride. They traveled through Raleigh, which was always busy. Wake Forest with its beautiful trees. Zebulon, which always seemed to be church quiet. They laughed at the rolling, wonderful feelings in the pits of their stomachs as they descended the hills of Highway 71.

This was the time that Beulah was in charge. She instructed her daughter to "make a squeeze" in the *colored* toilet at the bus station when they arrived in Wilson. Then they walked hand in hand to the little house on Queen Street where she and Wiley talked and Barbara Ann went to Louise's house to play with her best friend, James Earl.

But one day, Beulah went to Wilson alone. Barbara Ann awoke too late. She woke up because the bed was wet. Junior had peed, and Aileen was in a frenzy. She stripped the bed and washed the linen. She scrubbed the mattress with Clorox and Tide. Through her wrath, Barbara Ann and Jr. felt alone and lost. Aileen was on a rampage. Jr. was guilty and ashamed, and Barbara Ann was trying to defend him in the absence of their mother. Aileen fussed and cussed for what seemed like all day long.

"I just don't understand it. Folks get married. That means they grown! 'Sposed to handle their own business. But no, no, no, no! They bring it in here on me. And don't even care. Like I get all my shit for free. Hell, I work! I work hard for my mess! Ain't nobody give me a goddamn thing. And folks think they can just come in here and ruin my stuff! I will not have it! I just won't have it."

Holding each other, the children listened to the swooshing of the washing machine, the purring of the rollers as Aileen squeezed the water out of the sheets, the clicking of the pulley when she hung them out to dry on her continuous clothesline. She slammed the hatchet into the neck of a chicken with vengeance. She slammed cabinets and pots and pans when she started to cook spinach, which the children hated. And when Beulah finally came back, Aileen said to her,

"These are very expensive sheets. You need to whip that boy. I am not going to let him ruin my lovely things."

Beulah did not whip Jr. Instead, they all boarded the bus the next morning and went back to Wilson. Back to Queen Street, and back to Wiley.

●

He was glad to have his family back. "I promise not to ever hit you again," he said.

"Good. 'Cause I can't stand it. I just can't stand it."

"Well, you need to stop doing things to make me hit you."

"Things like what? Are you trying to say that it's my fault that you can't control your temper?"

"Yeah. You do stuff that drives me crazy."

"Well... that's a short trip."

"Beulah...." His lips became a thin line and the muscles in his cheeks twitched.

"Okay. Okay. What do you want me to change?"

"For one thing, you run your mouth too damned much. You talk about shit you don't even know. Always trying to make me look stupid."

"When did I ever do that?"

"All the time. I'm the man. I'm the boss around here. Just 'cause you got a good education don't make you smarter than me."

"So, what am I supposed to do? Just sit here and cower under you?"

"That's right."

She thought about that for a long time. Maybe she did see him as stupid because he was uneducated. She had caught him in so many lies she had lost faith in him. Still, she had no place else to go. She had to figure out a way to keep him happy. She remembered her promise to God, and she weighed her alternatives. She could either break her promise and run the risk of going to hell, or she could stay with Wiley and secure her place within the Pearly Gates. She chose the latter. Life on Earth is temporary. Her Heavenly home would last throughout eternity. The more she suffered here on Earth, the greater her reward in Heaven. God would take her right by the hand and guide her through it. Wiley was not trying to save his soul; she *was* trying to save hers. And she would live the rest of her life clinging to the faith that when she died, she could rest in peace.

"Okay," she said.

Things worked well for a little while after that. She had a way with him. Whenever she felt a rampage coming, she would say to him, "All right. Calm down. I'll do what you say if you get in a better mood."

Then one day Beulah and Mamie Wilson from across the street sat on the porch swing talking. They were thumbing through a Sears Roebuck catalog. The "wish" book they called it. Beulah licked her forefinger as she turned each page. Wiley was in the kitchen cooking. He called her to him three, maybe four times to help him find something. On the last trip she said, "You cook more than I do. You ought to know where everything is."

He ignored her comment. "What you and Mamie

gossiping about out there now?"

"Nothing. We are not gossiping. Just looking through the catalog. That's all."

"Uh huh."

She returned to the porch and thought nothing of it. But Wiley was steaming—sweating from the heat of the kitchen and furious that she could sit on the porch while he did her job. He was cooking turnip greens, and once he had them boiling in a pot, he moved to the front of the house to listen to Beulah and Mamie talk.

Their conversation floated seamlessly from the items in the book to a woman who lived nearby.

"I saw this same dress last week," Beulah said.

"I did, too" Mamie said. "Hattie Mae had it on when she came through here last week with her little raggedy children trailing behind her."

"Oh yeah. I feel sorry for them. Hattie Mae is always dressed to kill, and her kids look like little ragamuffins. Look like they don't get enough to eat. Poor little things."

"How many kids she got?"

"Three. I hear tell she's getting ready to have another one."

"Come on. She ain't got no husband. Ain't nobody ever even seen her with a man. How she get so many children?"

"Doggone if I know. But somebody's doing something."

They laughed. Wiley stormed to the front porch and threw a lemon at Beulah. It hit her in the face and broke her glasses. Then he grabbed her by her hair and dragged her into the house. Mamie followed. He threw Beulah on the bed and as she scrambled to get away, he caught her foot and dragged her to him. He slapped her several times, not a real beating as he had done before she moved to Durham, but he showed her that he was the boss. That much is certain. He said, "I told you...you run your mouth too damned much." And then he walked away. She sat up on the bed crying. Her nose was bleeding, and her legs trembled. Mamie said, "Well, Beulah, I'll see you later, hear?"

Beulah taped her glasses with surgical tape, and by supper they were kissing.

This rage in him would surface every so often, and Beulah had almost learned how to predict it. It was like a silent storm within him that no one could figure out. It started to happen elsewhere, even on his job. The foreman chastised him for being distracted.

"You need to pick up your step, boy. We got deadlines to meet."

Wiley said, "Who the hell you calling a boy? I'm just as white as you is!"

"Wiley, I don't know why you are so angry, but I have to live and work with these fellows. They don't like the way you talk to them."

"They need to learn how to respect me. I am not dumb like everybody think. I have a lot of shit on my mind."

"I can see that. I like your work, but if you don't straighten up, I'm going to have to let you go."

"Fine with me. I was looking for a job when I found this one. I can always find me some work."

The foreman fired Wiley that day, and he spread the word that Wiley was insubordinate. He could not find work anywhere in the greater Wilson area.

Beulah took a job at Jimmy Dempsey Laundry.

Eighteen

When Beulah went to work, her mother agreed to watch Wiley Jr. during the day. He was a nervous child as a result of the way his father treated him. This nervousness usually manifested itself in a wet bed, which infuriated Wiley and caused Beulah to endure some kind of physical or verbal abuse. Josephine's house was so quiet one could hear the ticking of the clock on the wall. Jr. needed that quiet to keep him calm and out of trouble. Besides, his other grandmother did not like him. She could not brag on him the way she could for Barbara Ann. His dark skin made her think that he was not really her grandchild. While she preferred very dark men for herself, black children were repulsive to her. They had no energy in them, no light. They reminded her of Starkey and his willingness to settle for simple *existence*. No real living at all, just work day in and day out with no progress.

But she adored Barbara Ann. She bought shoes and clothes for her, and she gave the child money. In contrast to Josephine, Easter's house was loud and full of loud people making merriment. There was music, dancing men and women, cigarettes and liquor, but only when Dave was not at home. He worked the swing shift now, so during the days when he was at work, Easter continued her business as usual, but she made sure everyone was gone by four in the afternoon. When Dave worked the night shift, she did the same thing. Her hours of operation coincided with his work schedule. In this way she could maintain her lifestyle without depending on him. It was not even reasonable for him to make her give up her business. She had asked him one time and one time only for help in paying a bill. When he refused to give her money she said to him, "Shit, *nigger*, the light bill is due." The smirk on his face let her know that he wanted her to beg. He wanted to control her, and *that*, for Easter Cooper Williams, would never happen. She would not ask him for money again.

Easter and Barbara Ann were very close. She taught the girl how to cook and serve food. They spent many long hours talking about family history. She told the child about her mother and father and the ways they died.

"Grandma, *you* had a mama?!"

"Sure I did. You think I was born your grandma?"

"Uh huh."

"Everybody has a mama, Sugar. And a daddy, too. Just like you. When my daddy got killed, we went to see my granny. She offered us lemonade, but my mama wouldn't take it. I could not believe how black she was, my grandma I mean. Tall and sturdy and cold-hearted, *black*. My mama, though, she was real pretty. She had long, long hair and big fat legs. She was colored, but most people couldn't even tell. Her daddy was white and so was mine, but her mama was black as hell, like your brother.

"How come he so black, Grandma?"

"I don't really know, Shug. Guess that's the way God wanted him, I reckon."

"You think my mama is ever going to have another baby? Like a girl, maybe?"

"Oh, I don't know. You never can tell."

"Where do babies come from?"

"Did you ask your mama that question?"

"Yes, Ma'am."

"What did she say?"

"She said I should stay in my little girl place."

"But you feel comfortable asking me?"

"Yes, Ma'am"

"Why?"

"I don't know. You told me a lot of secrets. I thought maybe you would tell me this one."

Easter looked at the wonder in the child's eyes. "It's not a secret," she said. "It has to start with two people who love each other."

"Oh."

Barbara Ann lowered her head and cried.

"What's the matter, child?"

"My mama and daddy fight all the time."

"I'm so sorry to hear that. Come on over here and sit down with me."

They sat in the rocking chair and Easter held Barbara Ann on her lap. "You know…it ain't got nothing to do with you, right?"

"Yes Ma'am."

"Then why do you cry about it?"

"'Cause it makes me feel bad. I get scared and I try to make them stop. Yesterday I told my daddy, 'Please don't hurt my mama!' and he got mad at me."

"Would you like me to speak with him about it?"

"Yes Ma'am, would you?"

"Sure. Don't you worry about it anymore, okay?"

"Okay."

Easter rocked the child to sleep. She wasn't particularly fond of Beulah, but this little angel was too precious to suffer like this. Easter would have to speak to her son and tell him to be careful about what he let the children see. She was certain that there were times when Beulah needed her ass kicked, but to do it in front of this child was unforgivable.

●

It was the summer of 1954. Dave was on the evening shift. The house was filled with lively, happy people. At 8:30 in the evening, Easter was frying the last batch of fish. The folks had to be gone by ten so she would have time to clean up before Dave arrived at midnight.

But something was wrong. All day long she had felt a queasiness in her stomach, a premonition of sorts, like something terrible was about to happen. She was very careful in her duties that night. She sensed a feeling of absolute despair for no reason. She went outside and looked up at the man in the moon. Even he looked sad. The air was still and silent. Not even the birds or crickets made a sound. Her clients noticed the difference in her.

"What's the matter, Easter? You sick?"

"No. I just have a funny feeling. Like something ain't quite right." She breathed deeply. "Ah," she said. "I'm sure it's nothing. Y'all go 'head and finish up. You gotta get out of here."

She heard the front door open. "We're closed," she yelled from the kitchen.

Dave came through the door and glared at her. He looked around the great room at the people sitting there. "I thought we put an end to all this," he said.

Easter's mouth dropped open. "What are you doing here?"

"I live here, bitch!"

"Bitch? Who you talking to?"

"Talking to you! Why are they here?"

"They're here because I invited them."

"How long has this been going on?"

"Ever since you stopped giving me your paycheck. Didn't you notice that the lights are still on? Didn't you notice the gas and water bill still got paid? You got so you don't do shit around here except sleep!"

She was unaware of the position of her hand on her hip. She pointed her finger at his face. "You, Mister, need to learn some responsibility."

He hit her and knocked her down. She got up swinging. They fought in front of all the people there. Easter ran to the kitchen and got a knife. Dave grabbed her arm and twisted it behind her back. Nobody did anything to help her; she had told them to stay out of it when the two of them fought. They had learned that lesson well because if one tried to intervene, to get between them or call the police, Easter would attack him directly. So, at first, they did nothing. But then it became obvious that this was not just a fight. Easter said, "I give! I give!" But Dave looked like a demon, like he was afflicted with some kind of evil spell. The whites of his eyes were blood red. Sweat poured from his forehead. He kept hitting Easter, even after she surrendered. The blows were methodical, intended to inflict great pain. He punched her in the kidneys, ribs, head and face. The men tried to stop him, finally, but by then it was too late. He kept hitting Easter. He beat her and beat her until her blood splattered all over him and she was unconscious.

Afterwards, Dave went to the bathroom and washed her blood off. The men rushed Easter to Mercy hospital. She never woke up. She died the same way her father had died, beaten to death by someone close to her.

This knowledge affected Barbara Ann for the rest of her life. She could not fathom the intensity of passion and hatred that was involved in killing someone with one's own hands. Perhaps the greatest horror for her lay in the fact that nothing happened to Dave. He was not arrested. He was not punished by the community. Black on black crime was not serious enough to compel an investigation. After Easter's funeral, Dave slipped quietly out of town as easily as he had slithered in, and Barbara worried, worried, *worried* that the same thing would happen to her mother.

Nineteen

Before she married, Beulah worked at the Ritz Theater where she sold tickets for the movies. It was glamorous. She dressed up every night and wore lipstick. She met interesting people and, of course, she was able to watch all the shows that came through Wilson during that time. The Ritz was a *colored only* one-story downtown establishment. The Drake and the Carolina Theaters were both uptown and two-story, with a balcony that had a side entrance so that Negroes would not interact with the whites. It cost a dime, but one could go in there and sit all day long watching the news, the movie, the previews and then doing it all over again if one chose to do so. The Ritz, on the other hand, only had two shows per night, so Beulah was usually home by eleven. She walked to work, but Shird always picked her up so that she would not have to travel the dark streets alone. The job did not pay very well, but it required very little energy and the tips were abundant. The money kept her supplied with her feminine incidentals—lipstick, vanilla, Dixie Peach and Jergens. She kept herself primped and proper. The seams of her stockings were always straight, and her long, narrow feet, accented by her high heel shoes, complimented the swish of her skirt at the top of her calf. The Sherrod girls were all beautiful, and she saw herself as the prettiest one. All this, her work ethic and her appearance, combined with the fact that she had a brilliant mind, would secure her admission to North Carolina Central and the promise of a bright and exciting future.

Now, as she walked the two-mile trek to Jimmy Dempsey Laundry, she reflected on the way her life had turned. Nothing was going according to plan. She had to report to work by seven in the morning, which meant she left home at six. Most of the time it was still dark, and although she made sure her children were awake, she knew they would go back to sleep as soon as she left. So, she wrote out instructions for them. Barbara Ann had to make the beds and wash the dishes; Junior had to take out the trash and empty the slop jar.

Beulah made a pot of coffee every morning and filled a mayonnaise jar with it to take on her trip. Often, she would stop for a tenderloin biscuit at Godwin's Café just before she arrived at work. Her lunch was leftovers from the night before and as soon as she reached the laundry she would place it on the flat iron. By noon it was as hot as a freshly cooked meal.

The irony of her employment did not escape Beulah. She absolutely hated doing laundry; now she did it for a living. She was the one who received the baskets of dirty garments right off the truck. She was the one who sorted through them, separated the whites from the colors, determined what needed to be starched and ironed and what could be rough dried. She pinned together socks and underwear, sent bloody sheets to the soaking area and tagged those items that needed hot or cold water. But the good news was that she had adult co-workers with whom she could talk, and Beulah loved to talk. She could talk over the loud machinery, and she worked hard all day long. It wasn't that she necessarily wanted everyone in her business; she just needed to say things out loud that she could not say at home. Wiley kept her stifled, careful about the things she could say. At work, however, she was free to speak her mind. So, she talked, and if one would occasionally answer her or comment on what she said, it would start the same conversation that had occurred the day before and the day before that.

"Wiley, he don't eat no peas and beans. I have to work. He gets mad if I don't bring him a steak. Me and the kids can eat anything. Chicken necks and macaroni. But he has to have a steak. I like the bony parts of a chicken myself. Not him. He got ulcers real bad. So, he has to be careful what he eats. What y'all think about that woman who wouldn't give up her seat on the bus? She sure started some mess, didn't she? White folks 'round here won't put up with that. Oh! Did y'all hear about Leroy? Yeah. The police got him last week and almost beat him to death! My daughter is nine years old and in the fifth grade! I had to take her out of Catholic school. Tuition went up to seven dollars a month! Lord have mercy. That's a whole week's rent. I'm so proud of her I'm 'bout to bust wide open! She got funny ways, though. Just like her damn daddy. Tell a lie in a minute. Oh! Let me get my things together. It's time to get off. Looks like it wants to rain. I have to stop in town and get Wiley a new shirt."

Whether or not her co-workers replied, Beulah never knew or cared. She would carry on by herself until she focused on something else to do. She could talk like that without interfering with her job, and she earned herself the reputation of being *mouthy.*

Mr. Dempsey liked her work. She started out at seventy-five cents an hour, but after three months she earned a ten-cent raise. It was enough to keep her supplied with coffee and buy potatoes for the week, and it paid the rent. In those days there were no signed leases for Negro tenants. If one did not pay the rent on Friday, there would be a notice on her door on Monday. If she did not pay by the following Friday, the sheriff would come and set her stuff on the street. Beulah made sure she paid her rent first. She went to work every single day to make sure the rent was paid. Neither sickness nor the weather could stop her. Rain, sleet, hail and brutal heat were all challenges that encouraged her to continue working her way into Heaven.

Even when Hurricane Hazel hit the Carolinas in October of 1954, Beulah went to work. It started as a simple, heavy rain. She bundled her coat and fought the wind as it turned her umbrella inside out. By evening the rising water reached her ankles as she trudged homeward. Already she had begun to sneeze. The storm hit hard that night and it raged along the Atlantic coastline leaving death and debris in its trail. The howling wind rocked the house. It shattered windows, uprooted trees and hurled garbage cans onto the roofs of surrounding houses. The horrible sounds awoke the children, and they ran into Beulah's room and cuddled with her. They were all afraid, but she covered their heads with the quilt and prayed all night.

By morning the storm had calmed as it moved northward all the way to Canada. Beulah and the children went out to assess the damage. Neighbors were in the street, too, talking about the intensity of the storm and praising God for the fact that no one was seriously hurt.

Beulah had just bought a television set, a kind of early Christmas present for her children. Before she got it they all went to Josephine's house to watch TV. There were many families that did not yet have a television, and Beulah's choice to buy one represented her idea of progress. Booker T. had given her one, but after a month, his wife made him go back and get it. By then the children were addicted to the shows they watched, and they would stay up until the stations went off, so Beulah went to the finance company and borrowed money to buy them one of their own. Of course, sometimes they would fall asleep trying to make sure they saw everything. The noise of the "snow" awoke them, and their eyes were red as fire pokes.

It was a new thing. A brand-new culture that kept them abreast of the things that were happening in the rest of the world. It was something upon which they could build dreams. The children laughed when they watched *Amos and Andy,* applauded the acts on the *Ed Sullivan*

Show, and made fun of Minnie Pearl on *The Grand Ole Opry.* Minnie Pearl's biggest attraction was the price tag on her hat, but the children loved to hear her say, "How-dee. I'm just so proud to be here!"

They never fought over what to watch; there were only three channels anyway. Beulah didn't care at all; she'd curl up and go to sleep by seven o'clock. Wiley, however, made demands when Douglas Edwards presented the evening news. When they heard the voice, "Good evening, everyone from coast to coast," the children knew they had to become extremely quiet, or they would be in serious trouble.

But the storm blew the antenna clean off the house, and it broke into little pieces. The children were devasted. The picture was snowy; the sound was garbled. Jr. wrapped the rabbit ears with aluminum foil, and it got better. Every so often he'd have to go over and move the ears here and there, or give the TV a whack, but for the most part, it worked like that throughout the rest of their childhood.

The most extensive injury to the neighborhood was to the school. Sam Vick Elementary. The winds had peeled back the roof and opened the building like a can of sardines. They did not go to school on the first day, but by evening of the second day there was a notice in *The Wilson Daily Times,* which intimated that all Vick students would go to Elvie Street for half a day until the roof was repaired. Since most parents worked during the day, and they needed the school to care for their children, this was a workable solution for what could have been an annoying and expensive problem.

Flora lived right down the street from Elvie. As Barbara walked to school every day, she developed a habit of stopping in to see her aunt either before she went to school, or when her day was over. Flora always fed her something. That was her way—always good at heart. Always willing to share. She was sweet and generous, and the child loved—*worshipped!*—a bowl of black-eyed peas and a biscuit. The habit became so strong that one day when Barbara went to her house and Flora was not quite finished cooking, the girl had the audacity to peep into her pot. Flora caught her. The child smiled and rubbed her stomach. "Ummmmmm," she said.

Flora folded her arms and frowned. "Barbr'ann...you see all these children I have to feed?"

"Yes, Ma'am."

"Well, I'm a little short today. Your mama and daddy don't give me anything to help out, and I need to feed my children first."

Flora paused a little then and Barbara lowered her head in shame. Then she added, "But there is one thing I want you to remember. Don't ever look into my pot again. That's impolite. You hear?"

"Yes, Ma'am. I hear." Her feelings were hurt, and she cried, but she learned that painful lesson that day, and she never forgot it.

●

In the spring of the following year Barbara got a job at Shackleford's Grocery. Sally Shackleford had just had a baby, and she hired Barbara to help out a little so she could go home and take care of her child and start dinner. Her house was right next door to the store. She paid the child fifty cents a week—an hour a day, five days a week after school.

Barbara went home one day to find her father standing by the window on the side of the house. He put his finger to his mouth to warn her not to tell. She went inside and Beulah and Louise were talking. Louise was Beulah's best friend, and the mother of James Earl. It was a warm, spring day and the window was open. Knowing that her father was listening to their conversation, Barbara tried to get her mother's attention and make her stop talking. She cleared her throat and shuffled her feet. She even raised her hand, but her attempts to be recognized were ignored. Beulah was complaining about Wiley.

"He don't eat no peas and beans," Beulah said. "He

come home today with a T-bone steak, and he think he done something. He don't think about sugar and flour and eggs. He buys cigars and then he pisses away the rest of his money. I have to take mine and pay bills. Buy groceries. Them weeks he don't make no money, I have to go begging to the finance company or to my mama. She sitting over there on all that money and she don't want to help me none because I got him."

Barbara coughed. When Beulah finally looked up the child pointed her head towards the window. Beulah did not get the hint. Louise shook her head.

"He makes me sick! I pray for him all the time."

Just then Wiley charged into the room and jumped on Beulah. He started hitting her with all his might. Louise yelled, "Stop! Wiley, stop it!"

He did stop hitting her then, but the things he said hurt worse.

"You a stupid bitch! I can't do nothing in this town because I'm saddled down with you. You jinky-assed witch! It's a thang *outcheah*, and to think that my kids have to suffer because they mama's so goddamned *stupid.*"

With that, he stormed out of the house. He stood on the front porch and shouted all kinds of expletives. "I want y'all to know the kind of wife I got in here," he said. "I'm mad all over!"

While he must have thought he was asserting his manhood so all the neighbors could see and hear, Louise said to Beulah, "I 'clare...you sure are a good one."

And Beulah settled into the comfortable role of victim.

Twenty

WHEN WORK WAS SCARCE IN THE SOUTH, PEOPLE GENERALLY headed north of the Mason-Dixon line. In the early 1900s they left the agrarian south in droves seeking industrial work in Philadelphia, Chicago and New York. The same thing happened in the fifties and sixties. With the Civil Rights Movement in full force, it was frequently difficult for the average day laborer to find enough work to support his family. Hopes of gainful employment lured men and women to the North. Sometimes they were successful, especially if there was a relative or friend waiting and willing to assist. There were times, however, that dreams were deflated when one took a chance and made the sojourn blindly. The city was new to him or her. The people were distant, cold. Brutal winters brought on unexpected illnesses like pneumonia and bronchitis. With no real education and absolutely no money, the failures were abysmal. Reports of hard times channeled through the gossip circuit like a flash flood. "I heard he got locked up for stealing milk off of people's porches." The shame prevented the offender from going back home.

To eliminate extra baggage like family, police records, and debt, the traveler would often change his name. In this way he could start over and use his past experiences as life's lessons that could guide him in what not to do in his new environment. This duplicity rarely caused a problem. It was easy to get a new social security card, and the new identity protected him. In the event of a bad marriage or too much other responsibility, his Southern family could never find him and make him accountable.

In most of these cases the men left their wives and children at home while they searched for a better place. That was at least the promise as they packed a suitcase or a plastic bag in preparation of boarding a train. This is the way it happened to Wiley and Beulah. He had not worked on a regular basis in three years; she was the one who supported the household. They sat in the front room one afternoon in October of 1958.

"I want you and the kids to come with me," he said.

"No. Not right now."

"Why do you always do that?"

"Do what?"

"Dispute my word. Defy me."

"I'm not trying to do that. I don't want to go all the way up there and starve while you look for work. We gonna be all right. You go ahead. I got a job. Barbr'ann got a job. At least we can eat and have a place to stay. You go on. Don't worry about us."

He had hoped she would say that. His plans for the future did not include her. He harbored a secret that he could never discuss with her. So, he kissed her good-bye, walked to the train station, and headed towards Washinton, D.C.

Now Beulah was both married and single at the same time. With him gone she was the boss. She went to work, and she went to church. Once in a while she would stop in to see her mother or one of her sisters without worrying about reporting her every move to Wiley. Her children helped with housework, and they prepared meals. She could sleep without worry of interruption in the middle of the night. And she could talk all she wanted without expecting a slap in her face. Her friends gave her canned peanut butter, and her brother had brought her a cord of scrap wood, enough to last through the winter. The wood was shaped in wedges as if someone cut a circle from a large plank and left the edges for whoever wanted to pick it up and carry it away. She was set. She was not going to give up her little protective unit to go traipsing off with him when he had already proved himself to be unreliable.

But something wasn't right. She started to get sick. She had no energy, and she felt bad all the time. She lost weight, and she lost teeth. During this time, she had long conversations with her daughter about what to do in case she died. It was necessary to instruct the girl on how to take care of Wiley Jr, where to find the insurance policy, and where she wanted to be buried. The thought of death plagued her, and the delicious tears flowed freely as she anticipated leaving her children to fend for themselves. Her legs were tired and weak all the time, and her belly swelled. She was convinced that she had a tumor that would soon terminate her life, and she wanted to make sure that everything was ready.

"I want to be buried in that white dress," she told Barbara. "I don't know how to get in touch with your daddy, so everything is going to be left up to you. He wouldn't have enough sense to handle it anyway. Now, there's not going to be anything left from the insurance; it's just enough to put me in the ground. You will have to work and take care of your little brother, you hear?"

"Yes, Ma'am."

They hugged and cried through the night, and Barbara took on the task of caring for her dying mother.

Wiley did not return until February of the following year. He had not sent any money, but Beulah was glad to see him. She could tell him that she was dying, and he would have to take care of the children. He was surprised at what he saw, a frail little thing that looked nothing like the girl he had married. He was on a mission, but he had to withhold it until he found out what was wrong with her.

"You have to go to the doctor," he said. "Let's go *now*."

She surrendered. Hand in hand they walked to the

corner of Green and Pender streets. Beulah was terrified. She had found solace in not knowing, but the tumor moved from time to time, and she considered that it might be affecting her heart and liver. When Dr. Hines finished examining her, Beulah and Wiley held hands in the waiting room for him to give them the results.

"I am so scared," she told Wiley.

"Don't be scared until we find out what it is."

"What if he can't fix it?"

"We will worry about that when the time comes. Don't worry, baby. I'm going to stay right here with you."

In his heart he meant that. He really did love her. There was no way he could tell her that the American Dream had failed him. No way could he tell her that he was living in abject poverty in D.C. There was plenty of work in the city, but very little for a man who could not read or navigate a blueprint. He had no car, so he had to rely on public transportation. Sometimes the bus came on time; sometimes it didn't. He was often late for work, and this caused him to get fired several times. Until he made this trip, he had not been able to afford the train ride back to Wilson, but he had left in such a huff and with such determination to show Beulah and everybody else that he was better off without her, he would not have gone back there, anyway. He could not accept the notion that he may be inadequate. But now, for the first time in their married life, she needed him, and he could not abandon her in her time of need.

He was glad she had not come to D.C. The real reason he had left would have been too much for her to handle. But his thoughts lingered there where the woman he had hoped to marry waited patiently. *She* had been their babysitter when she was sixteen. They had a child in 1954, a child they had left with an elderly couple in Virginia to keep that secret away from Wilson. Now, she was pregnant again, and her parents had disowned her. Wiley was all she had left. They made plans to marry once he divorced Beulah, but now, well...now, he may not need a divorce. Beulah was dying, and as cold as it sounded, even to him, her death would solve all his problems.

He held her tightly as Dr. Hines motioned them into his office. He pulled out the chair for her and made sure she was comfortable.

"Well, Beulah," Dr. Hines began. "There is nothing seriously wrong with you." He wore a smile that seemed to cover his entire face. "Congratulations. You are going to have a baby."

The smile faded from the doctor's face as he watched the couple in front of him process that information. It was like the moon had collided with Earth and left them suspended in time. They did not say anything for a small eternity, and then Beulah exclaimed, "Wh—what--? What did you say?"

"I said you are expecting a baby in the middle of July."

Wiley stood up. "Goddamn!" he said. He charged out of the doctor's office dragging Beulah along with him.

The walk home was a long one. Wiley cussed and fussed the whole way.

"Junior is eleven years old. Ain't no way in hell a man can be with a woman for eleven years and nothing happen, then boom! All of a sudden she big. I know you been fucking around with somebody else. I ain't even been here. Who is it?"

He had no idea that she was as surprised as he was. It made no sense. At thirty-two years old, a baby never entered her mind.

"Wiley, I swear…as God is my witness—"

"Fuck God!"

"I didn't do nothing."

"Oh, you did something all right. I'm going to stay here until I find out. Then I am going to kill you. I got me somebody. Oh yeah. I got me somebody in Washington. I'm gonna kill your ass. Then I'm gonna be with her."

They walked into the cold house. Beulah started to make a fire while Wiley raged. He was not paying attention. She had a wedge of wood in her hands when he reached for her. She swung around and hit him with the wood on the bridge of his nose. It immediately blackened both his eyes. The look on his face showed that she had caught him off guard. She was willing to defend herself this time. She was willing to fight him back. She hit him with that wood on his shoulder, his back, his neck.

"I knew it!" she cried. "All this time. All this time! You been whipping on me and accusing me. I knew it! You beat on me, and I forgave you. You piss away our money and I forgave that too. I knew you had somebody, and I can even forgive that!" She landed a blow across his kneecap, and he went down. She stood over him pointing the wedge at his face. "But I cannot forgive what you just said about God. Don't you dare blaspheme up in this house!"

Beulah threw the wood into the stove and then she sat down and crossed her legs. "If you had any sense you would know. The doctor said the baby is coming in July. Count backwards nine months. I got like this in October. You were *here* in October."

Wiley scrambled to his feet and ran to the mirror. The sight of his image frightened him. Nobody had ever put a mark on him. It surprised him that this woman he had whipped like a child for so many years was ready and willing to hurt him. He was too pretty to take the blows that he determined to put on her, so he backed away. He ran outside and threw rocks at the house.

Now, he faced a dilemma: two women pregnant, both due in July. Which one would he choose? Trying to feed a family on the pitiful scrapings of employment he could find was not even possible. It was hard enough to try to feed his own face. His only hope lay in the fact that both women worked.

His girlfriend came and went as she pleased. She had an apartment in Maryland. She was his only staple. When he couldn't afford to eat, she fed him. She nursed his wounds when he told her he had been mugged in Wilson. It didn't bother her that he could not give her nice things; he was all she wanted. Young, strong and hard-working, she never complained about anything. She understood his need to visit his other family, and she shared her money with him. Eventually, through her job, she met someone who helped Wiley get a position that only required his drywall plastering skills. He did not need to read or write.

He moved into her apartment in Silver Spring, Maryland. He bought a red Pinto, and he became a two-family man. With a decent place to live, reliable transportation, and a supportive woman, he now believed he could conquer the world. But he needed to be really careful with Beulah.

Part Five

Barbara

Twenty-One

THIS IS AWKWARD. I AM UNCOMFORTABLE TALKING ABOUT myself in third person. Making the transition, though, defies everything I have learned about *traditional* writing. My friend and mentor, the late Ron Gottesman, once told me, "Until you do it, nothing has been done." His spirit still lingers in my soul. So, I am taking a leap in the faith of that line here, and I confess that I am Barbara.

Both of my parents are dead now. My brother is dead, and my sister and I live far apart. But I think of them all often. I dream about them, and I try to come to some kind of definition of love based on my experiential knowledge of it and them.

Mama died in August of 2008. She developed pancreatic cancer that eventually spread to all her organs. She designed and orchestrated her own funeral. My sister and I tried to follow her directions to the letter—the dress she wore, the colors of the flowers, where she would be buried. For the three years prior to her death, I had sent money every month. She used most of it to pay the expenses involved in her going home celebration. She was eighty-one years old.

There was standing room only at Rountree Missionary Baptist Church on the day of Mama's funeral. So many people had such wonderful things to say about her and her involvement in the church community. Her former employers sent flowers, and Congressman G. K. Butterfield sent a letter of recognition.

Her life had been a hard one. The last time I saw her alive, she asked me to convince the doctor to send her to The Brian Center. That was where she wanted to spend her last days; she did not want to go home to my father. So much had happened, and I understood completely her desire to be free of him.

He, on the other hand, was just as determined to be by her side. While I was in Wilson, I called to check on him. "Can you take me to see Mama?" he said. I promised to pick him up in an hour, and when I arrived, he stepped out on the front porch *clean!* He wore a white shirt that was open at the collar, tan slacks, brown, gleaming leather shoes, and a Kangaroo cap. He looked like he was going on a date.

"Dude!" I said. "You mighty sharp."

"Hell yeah...I'm going to see my baby!"

Their visit was uncomfortable for me and too long for her. Whenever she caught him looking away, she would stare at me and jerk her head towards the door.

Finally, I said, "We have to go, Dad. The nurse says that visiting hours are over."

It was a lie, and I think he knew it, but he kissed Mama on her forehead and reluctantly left the room.

I took him to lunch at Parker's and then we went for a drive through Pinetops and Tarboro. "This is my old stomping ground," he said. "Girl, you have really given me a treat today. When I was a young man, me and my buddies used to chase tail all around these parts. Now...I done fucked around and got old. I 'clare...it's a thang. But we had us some *good* times all through here."

He tossed his head back and laughed.

We drove for a long time, circling back around and coming through Rocky Mount and Sharpsburg on Hwy 301. For a moment he was very quiet, and then he picked up the tales of his youth. It was as if he were talking to himself.

I was lost for a minute. They messed up the roads so bad I didn't know where I was, but yeah, there's the path that leads to where we used to live. God—damn! Ain't been out here in a hunerd years. Heh, heh, heh. When I was a boy me and my buddies used to run down that path every Sunday. We'd play out here right by the road. Way after while somebody would holler, 'Here come a car!' And we would all run to the road to see it. Heh heh. We would stay out here all day on Sunday. Sometimes we'd see a car; sometimes we didn't. But that was the way we had fun, waiting for cars, shooting marbles and climbing trees. Ol' man Lassiter used to sit on his front porch and whittle swords out of fallen tree branches. He'd give 'em to us boys for Christmas or birthdays, you know. Er'body had one. We'd sword fight and eat our bologna sandwiches. Had us a ball all day. Life was so simple then. Wait...turn in right here!

He wanted to show me where his father was buried. I brought my truck to a complete stop and turned on my right blinker. It was a dirt road, filled with large rocks and deep dips. It was surrounded by tall trees and unmowed grass. We stopped and I helped him get out.

This is what they call a pauper's grave. When my daddy got sick, they took his whole rectum out. He was a good man. A good man. Worked hard all his life. Never had no money, but he worked like a dog until he got sick. When he died back in '67, the only place the family could afford was this piece of shit cemetery. Look at it. The weeds all grown up over the graves. I swear...it's a damn shame.

We didn't get along all that good. He didn't like me 'cause I was yellow, you know. I wasn't crazy 'bout him neither, 'cause he was so black. Black people don't even think like we do. I swear...it's a thang outcheah! You ask a nigger where he's goin' and he'll tell you where he's been...Mama's sick. You know that?

"Yes, Daddy, I know."

"Can you take me to see her?"

"We did that earlier today."

"Oh. Oh, that's right. I forgot."

He wrinkled his face and rubbed his brow. "So, your name is Barb, right? Where you live? You still in California?"

"No, Sir. I live in Texas now."

"Texas huh? Yeah…I been there. 'Bout how *fuh* is it from here to where you live now and from where you live now to where you used to live?"

It took me a moment to decipher that he was asking me the difference in mileage between North Carolina and Texas and Texas and California. And before I realized it, I answered, "'Bout the same *fuh.*"

"You doing all right out there?"

"Yes, Sir."

"You a teacher now, right?"

"Right."

"Yeah, yeah, yeah. That's right. Dr. Barb! Goddamn! When your picture was in the paper, my friends said, 'Wiley, we didn't think you were doing anything, and here you doing everything!' I was so proud. You leaving them little boys alone?"

"Most of the time." I knew he was in a lighter, joking spirit, so I added, "Sometimes I have to get their mothers to sign a permission slip."

I winked. He howled with laughter. That was our way. We could laugh and joke about things that my mother would surely deem inappropriate.

"Well, you might as well go on and get you a white man. You already been through 'bout a *hunerd niggers.*"

My father hated white people, so the comment was strange to me to say the least. But I had considered the notion. I helped him back to the truck. Once we were settled and back on the road I said, "So, it wouldn't bother you if I married a white man?"

"What the hell you talking 'bout, girl? Why would you ever want to do that?"

"You just said that I should get one."

"You's a *damn lie*! I would never say no shit like that!"

We drove in silence for the rest of the trip as I pondered the things my mother had told me about him. "He's mental," she'd say. "Night and day, hot and cold. You never know which way he's coming, so stay alert. Be ready to defend yourself. I think it's what you call a paranoid *schizophren.* One day last year he took off his belt and whipped your sister, right in front of her children. She turned around and said to him, 'Are you having fun?' That made him mad as hell. He took it out on me. Said I didn't raise her right. Said none of y'all respect him. You be real careful, you hear?"

Indeed, he had begun to show signs of some kind of dementia. It had never occurred to me that he was sick; I thought he was just plain mean. When I left him at the house he said, "You coming back tomorrow to take me to see Mama?" He looked so pitiful—like an abandoned and confused little boy. I put my arms around him.

"No, Dad. I am leaving tomorrow. I have to go back to work. I'll be back in a couple of months."

At the time I said that it was a lie. I had not planned to go back until Christmas. As it turned out, my mother died two months later.

At the wake and the funeral my father sat quiet, motionless, like a zombie. He just stared at Mama. She looked so pretty—prettier than I had seen her in such a long time. The years had not been good to her, and with the limitations of work and church as her only social life, she had not worn makeup in more than half a century. The funeral home personnel had rouged her cheeks and painted her lips. They curled her hair and spread it out on the pillow. She seemed to be at perfect peace. During the funeral ceremony, Reverend Barron stopped speaking to us and addressed Dad directly.

"Wiley, you all right?"

"Yeah. Yeah. I'm all right."

He held that demeanor, dazed and speechless, for two days. On the third day he said to me, "What you getting ready to do?"

"Ah…" I stumbled for words. "Nothing much. You need me to do something?"

"Will you take me to see Mama?"

Assuming that he wanted to go to the cemetery, I said, "Sure."

So, we got in my rental car and headed towards Rest Haven Cemetery on Lane Street. As I put on the blinker and entered the left lane, he said, "You going the wrong way. Mama's over there on Downing Street."

I don't think I have ever felt more pain. His eyes, wide and eager, peered into mine and I saw them cloud over. "Yeah, you right. Mama gone." His bottom lip trembled, and he started to cry. "I was so cruel to her. She was my baby, and I was cruel to her!" He looked upward. "Oh God! If I could just see her one more time, I'd tell her that I am sorry!"

He cried so hard that day. I didn't know what to say or do, so I said nothing. I held him in my arms and let him cry it out. Then I said, "Do you want to come to Texas and stay with me?"

"Naw…Hell naw. I'm gonna stay right here 'til Mama comes back."

I only visited with my father one more time after that. He had become too much for my sister to handle alone, so she called and asked me to come home. I went during Christmas break the following year. I could see that his condition was rapidly deteriorating. He had lost weight, and he was eighty-seven years old, but he still had that pimp daddy swag in his walk. Again, I invited him to move to Texas with me.

"I already told you I ain't going. I'm gonna die right here *IN-THIS-HOUSE* where Mama was."

The stubborn old mule. I could take care of him, I thought. But he proved to me that he could take care of himself. He cooked every day. He bathed and dressed himself every day.

What I did not realize at the time was that his plan was to die in the little house on the corner of Vick and Viola streets. It was the house I had watched Uncle Shird build with his own hands when I was a child. The house had become the cornerstone for Sherrod Village, and while it held many, many memories of Mama for both of us, it also was a kind of anchor home for me. When I was eleven, I worked there for the first tenants, the James family. I cooked and cleaned and took care of their three children. At the time the house had hardwood floors. There was a full bathroom, complete with a tub and shower and a kitchen that was large enough for a dining table. For me, that was a great luxury. I enjoyed cooking in that kitchen, and once in a while, when I had put the children down for their nap, I would sneak a shower in the bathroom.

Dad got sick early in the next year, and my sister had him admitted to the hospital. He was fighting mad for that. She called me again.

"Girl, he is so mad at me right now. They had to restrain him because he was trying to bite the nurses when they put in the IV."

"I know this is rough on you. I am so sorry you have to go through it alone."

"You don't know the half. Look...I went to see him yesterday and he was laying up there buck naked." She laughed. "I can see why the women all fought over him."

I laughed too. That was Wiley Williams, all right. Rebellious as hell and determined to have his way. "He probably thinks he's going to die," I said. "He's mad at you for putting him in the hospital because he wanted to die at home."

"He's not going to die," she said. "He's too damn mean and ornery to die."

"You might be right. I remember a time that he told me, 'When St. Peter comes to get me, I'm gonna tell him I can't go. I can't goooooo! Somebody's got to stay here and argue with this old woman.'"

She laughed so hard that day. And then she started to cry. I knew it was stressful for her. Our brother died in 1993, and I lived far away. She had borne the burden of taking care of our dying mother, and now she had to take care of Dad. On the one hand, it was only fitting; she was the only one he ever tried to parent and support. On the other hand, he *was* my father too, and I felt bad that she had to go it alone."

"I will come home on Spring Break and help you take care of him," I said.

"Okay. Thank you."

But the great Wiley Williams became the late Wiley Williams in February of 2010. It was just a year and a half after Mama's death. We did not have an elaborate ceremony. It was very simple and in the chapel of the funeral home. His brother Charlie delivered the eulogy.

Twenty-Two

Death, with all her mysteries, has a way of delivering truths and revelations even as she continues to harbor secrets. I am told that at my father's funeral at least three of my brothers were present. They never came forward to let my sister and me know, but one was from Charlotte, and I think I know who he was. The others are complete strangers, and I wish I had had a chance to meet them. There was one, though, who called while we were preparing for the funeral, and he told a story that was consistent with something my dad had told me many years ago. He explained why he was not coming to Wilson.

I ain't seen that motherfucker since I was nine years old. I live in Roanoke. Nothing's changed. He knew I was here. My mother was only sixteen years old when she got pregnant with me. Wiley brought her up here and, after I was born, they gave me to an old couple who raised me. I was born in 1950. Then, in 1958, my mother got pregnant again. By him. So, they came to get me. 'We gon' be one big happy family,' they said. But the folks who had become my parents would not let me go. So, Wiley and my mother stayed up this way until my brother was born. Me and you are half brother and sister, but my little brother and I are full blood. Anyway, they claimed they were going to get married and fight my parents in court. But Wiley went back to Wilson because your mother was sick. That's when he found out that your sister was on the way. Sonofabitch was slinging interstate dick. He and my mother never did get married, but they lived together in Maryland like husband and wife. After a few years, she made plans to marry somebody else, and Wiley went on back home to your mother. No. I am not coming to his funeral. Fuck him.

Now. We are indeed blood related, but I don't know this guy. I never met him. I was offended by his call. I truly understand his anger, and I will defend his right to say what he did with my dying breath. But this was my father this guy was low rating, and with all his faults, I did love Wiley Williams. I was glad this brother would not to come to the funeral.

●

I don't go to Wilson much anymore. When my parents died, they eliminated the reasons why I made the trip. Once in a while, though, I will go back for a family or class reunion. A few years ago, when both of those events occurred, I packed my bags and boarded a plane.

At first, I felt out of place, uneasy, like I did not belong there. I do not have great memories of my childhood the way most people do. Nor do I have relatives who would offer me a place to stay during my visit. Wilson no longer felt like *home.* My hotel was on the outskirts of town, about four miles west of the hotel that was reserved for Darden High School Alumni. So, I think I must have felt a little isolated because I did not recognize anyone I saw in the lobby. I was determined to go into town, into the familiar Sherrod Village.

As I drove my rental car through the streets of Wilson, I noticed that there were many changes. New restaurants and businesses. Shopping centers, housing developments, and heavy traffic. I headed east on Old Raleigh Road, turned right on Ward Boulevard, left on Tarboro, and right on Nash Street. It was a ritual I had developed over the years of going through downtown Wilson to get my bearings. Woodard's Barber Shop was still busy. Jackson Chapel Church was in the same place.

Once I crossed Pender Street, I began to get the feel of home. Most of the houses that I remember from my youth were still standing, although some of them had deteriorated and lost the dignity they used to hold. Others had sprung up anew in between those that were boarded up and overrun with weeds. When I reached the remnants of the majestic Vick Street, I observed the spot that used to be Brewington's Grocery, the Dixon and Bullock homesteads, the corner of Green and Vick streets where my cousin Staton lived on the southwest end and the Elliott family owned the house on the northeast. At Viola Street I turned right, and I stopped briefly to embrace the moment. Mama and Daddy had lived in the little house on the corner until they died. Uncle Shird's store was next to it. His house, Grandma Josephine's house, was next to that. Shird's son Otis still lives directly across the street and, truth be told, he owns—had inherited—just about every house on that block.

I was suddenly ten years old again. The ghost of Shird sneezing, working, complaining and talking loudly seemed to fill me with the spirit of home. I drove slowly up the street where I found Michael, Otis' brother, pushing a lawnmower as he prepared for his day's work.

"What's up, boy?" I said.

"Who dat? He took a closer look. "Barbr'ann! Girl, you lookin' good. When you get in town?"

"Last night."

"How long you gon' be here?"

"About a week. How are you doing?"

Of all the Artis/Sherrod descendants Michael had the most beautiful smile. It was pure joy to see him flash that boyish grin.

"I am doing well. So, are you on your way to work?"

"Yeah...got to get to it before it gets too hot."

"Good job. Well, don't let me keep you. I am sure I will see you again before I leave. Oh...by the way, do you know where I can find Toby Fitch?"

"What you want with Toby?"

"Now see...that's not your business. Do you know where I can find him or what?"

"Yep. Go look on the corner of Pender and Nash. He's there every day. That's right. You lookin' for Toby, that's where you gon' find him."

"Thanks. I'm going up here and rob Redlee of one of those beers. You have a good day, hear?"

"Yeah, okay. But what you want Toby for?"

I laughed and waved. I knew the suspense was killing him. Truth is, Toby was the young lawyer whose firm handled my divorce, and when I ran away from Wilson and was homeless in California, his family offered to pay my way back home. I declined that offer, but I wanted Toby to see that I was healthy, happy, and doing okay.

I drove across Reid Street and parked. Redlee was sitting on the porch. His name is Reginald Lee Simms, but with the propensity to call children by their first and middle names (Barbara Ann, James Earl, Mary Joyce), and the musicality of an eastern North Carolina accent, all of Wilson knows him as Redlee. He lost his leg to cancer a few years before, so his porch is wrapped with a ramp that accommodates his wheelchair. As I climbed the ramp to greet him, he showed a broad, but toothless grin, and after a hug and kiss on the cheek, he offered up a beer. It was only ten o'clock in the morning, but I expected to enjoy a beer with him, and since I was on vacation, I was not inhibited by time. We exchanged the usual *Hey! How you doing? I'm doing fine, fine,* and I noticed Otis coming up the hill with a big smile and gold tooth flashing in the sunlight. My oldest living friend, Shelia, lived across the street, and she came out to greet me. Before long the Parkers arrived: Solo and Joyce from Philadelphia, and Happy from Georgia. They brought their spouses and children. Redlee's sister Flora Darlene was there and his brother Larry Darnell, who lived in Indiana. The porch was crowded with longtime friends and relatives, and we howled with laughter as we told old lies and invented new ones. Darnell (as we generally called him) was the keeper of the beer, so when I asked him for another one, he said to me, "You can get anything Larry has to offer, baby."

The whole porch was electric with laughter, and it seemed that everyone had a comeback for that line: *Look who's talking shit...That boy never did have a lick of sense... Better watch out there now...You know she's educated...She gon' put some of that PhD shit on yo' ass.*

Darnell was also fully stocked with funny stories of our childhood days. He told a story about his brother Ronnie, the family rebel.

Daddy was getting ready for work one morning, and Ronnie had gotten in trouble the night before. So, Daddy told him not to leave the house. 'Bout eleven o'clock that morning, Ronnie went down to Uncle Shird's store. Well! Daddy came home at dinnertime and he said, 'Where's Ronnie?' I didn't want to get my ass kicked, so I told. Daddy said, 'Go tell him I said come here.' So, I went down the street and told Ronnie what Daddy said. He said, 'Daddy ain't home yet, boy, quit lying. It ain't but twelve o'clock.' I said, 'Okay...but I am not going back and tell him that I didn't see you.' Well...Ronnie took his time, and when he finally climbed the hill, Daddy was standing right there with the belt. This was before Viola was paved, you know. So, when Ronnie saw Daddy, he fell right down on his knees. He said, 'Daddy, please don't beat me. I'll give you everything I got.' So, Ronnie reached way down in his pocket, and when he brought his hand out, he laid that penny down on the ground. Daddy whupped...his...ass! He made Ronnie go upstairs and I'ma tell you the truth. Ronnie did not leave the house again for a whole week!

The family eased into tales of ass-whippings, and each one topped the other. Finally, I asked Darnell how he got to Wilson.

"Did you drive or fly?"

"No. I took the bus."

"From Indiana? That's a pretty long ride."

"Yep. 'Bout twenty hours usually. I was 'sposed to

get here Tuesday, but the bus broke down in Knoxville, Tennessee. We waited for almost a full day. Then the bus company put me in a taxi and brought me to Raleigh. So, I didn't get here 'til yesterday."

"A taxi? From Knoxville?!" There was general derision among the porch crowd.

"Yep."

Otis said, "Are you still high?"

Poor Darnell. He had to laugh at that himself. What he meant was that the passengers on the bus were boarded on shuttles that caught up with other buses that took them to their destinations. But the thought of a taxi from Knoxville, Tennessee to Raleigh, North Carolina created an image that none of us would ever forget. I know I am right about that.

●

In Wilson the porch is more than an attachment to a house. It is a monument, a symbol of community. Folks usually bring their morning coffee to the front porch so they can sit and observe the goings on in the neighborhood. They feel the freshness of the day and listen to the birds chirp. That's how everybody knows everybody else's business. One can see the cops coming, or the insurance man. You can talk about the weather with passersby or check out who is getting a new television. There are few secrets in a community, especially one as small as Sherrod Village. All the porches have furniture: a worn-out sofa, a couple of kitchen chairs. Seldom is there one with actual porch furniture, and when there is none at all, folks tend to sit on the steps. It used to be that conversations on the porch were limited to men; the women busied themselves in the house. If one of them approached the porch or even stood at the screen door, all talk stopped immediately, and she became the victim of inquisitive stares.

Nowadays, though, the porch is there for all to enjoy, and women have either earned the right or taken the privilege of participating in the banter that happens there.

After we wiped the tears of laughter that followed

Darnell's stories and Otis' comment, I focused on the house across the street next to Shelia. It was where I lived from age ten to grown. The trees needed to be trimmed, the grass was grown up around it, and the porch was falling apart. There were plywood boards where the windows and doors used to be, and the house looked as sad as an abandoned puppy. It was a place of precious memories for me. 903 E. Viola Street. It was there that I first fell in love. It was there that I paid the rent with my earnings from Wilson Variety Store. I lived there when I experienced my first kiss. It was in that house when I realized that I had the potential of being a thief. Miss Louise moved in with us at one point along with six of her children and her mother, Miss Dora. Miss Dora used to cook sausage, grits, eggs, and biscuits every morning and put them in the cabinet for her grandchildren. Almost every morning I would go into the kitchen and steal a piece of sausage and wrap it in a biscuit before putting it in my pocket.

The house held the memory of the first time I got drunk. I remember it was Christmas, and my friends and I shared a jar of white lightning that we cut with grape Kool-Aid. I was fifteen years old, and when I came into the house, I kicked the foot tub from one end of the hallway to the other. Miss Dora was standing right there, but instead of telling my mother on me, she laughed until she could hardly breathe because I said to the foot tub, "Excuse me."

Yes. The house harbored many, many memories, and now as I looked at it, I realized that the boards would have to be removed. The things that happened in and around that house were too precious to be contained. So much of my own history was there, and I needed to open it up, set it free, and allow it to blossom. I would have to find a way to do that.

Each day that I was in Wilson I managed to find my way to Redlee's porch. Sometimes he was at home; sometimes he was not. But I sat on that porch and watched the house across the street. I could almost hear Slim Short, Ted Hooker, Sepia Serenade, and Oral Roberts. I could smell my mother's coffee. I began to reminisce about the things that happened in that house. My mother used plastic curtains. My cousin Spencer had painted her room with pink calcimine on the morning of the day he died. I lived in that house when I joined the Patrol Force at school, when I became a debutante with Delta Sigma Theta Sorority, when I graduated from high school, when we brought my baby sister home from the hospital. I reflected on how I had survived shit most folks had never even thought about, yet it was those experiences that made me the woman I am now.

I looked for Toby Fitch every day, but he was never on that corner. I didn't really know why I wanted to see him so badly except to thank him for helping me get my divorce in '79. Now a Superior Court Judge, he was an intrepid young lawyer at the time, and over the years, he had been more than willing to answer any questions I had regarding legal matters. He was the only man for whom I had enough respect to follow his advice. I convinced myself that whatever it was I was looking for, Toby could and would guide me in the right direction.

I was finally able to reach him by phone on the last day of my visit.

"Barbara Williams! How the hell are you?"

"I am terrific. How are you?"

"Can't complain. I woke up this morning."

"Are you at home?"

"No…actually, I am on the street right behind my house. I'm getting my oil changed."

"Okay. I'll find you."

"Look for a white truck."

With that I made a bee line for the street behind Lodge Street. I had no trouble finding the elusive Milton Frederick "Toby" Fitch, Esquire.

Our conversation was short, but we exchanged phone numbers, and I promised to call him when I got back to Texas.

The little house on Viola Street consumed my thoughts during the entire flight home. I wanted to own it, rescue it, and make it a livable space again. I called Toby as soon as I got home.

"I want to buy the house across from Redlee."

"You used to live there, right?"

"Right. My parents never owned anything. The most they ever had in the bank was nine hundred dollars. In '74 my dad came home with a brand new red and white Cadillac, but Mama had to work and pay for it. Ha! She couldn't even drive; she was almost fifty when she learned how. They struggled with money issues all their lives. I just think it will be a great tribute to them both if I buy that house."

"Hold on a minute."

The phone was silent for about five minutes, but the screen showed that Toby was still on the line, so I continued to hold. When he returned, he said, "I just talked with the man who owns that property. You can get it for $8500."

I could hardly contain my excitement. "I want to fix it up, maybe use it as a summer home or a little space for writing. There is so much rich history in Wilson, and I want to write about it. I will probably return in late summer and try to find a contractor."

"I know a guy."

Afterword

TODAY I RECOGNIZE THAT MY LIFE HAS COME FULL CIRCLE. When I was a child, I was pitifully thin—hell—I was just plain skinny, and it was because I did not get enough to eat. My friends laughed at me. When I left my abusive husband, my friends laughed at my failure. At one time it cost twelve dollars to attend the Darden High School Alumni banquet, and I didn't have twelve dollars. My friends laughed again. But I came to realize that none of that matters. I can honestly say that I am a happy woman, and I have paid my dues to get here. I was reared in abject poverty. We did not have a telephone. I always had to share a room with my brother or some other relative, and I walked everywhere I went. Now, I own three houses and three vehicles. There is no brag here; it's just that I believe every generation should start where the last one ended and move forward. I have noticed that many of my contemporaries have progressed to the point that they leave East Wilson. I am guilty of that myself. The truly successful want to live in the multicultural area of West Wilson, or they move to another state, and in the process, they escape the depression of the place that gave them life. I want to lock in again and reconnect with my roots. Buying the property on Viola Street was my way of doing that.

My first book, *Sherrod Village,* tells the story of my journey to completion. I frequently encourage my students to write about themselves. One has to get to know the *self* before she can do anything. "Write yourself free," I tell them, and I believe that is what I have done here. We are all connected to something or someone who helps shape us into what we become. The choices we make guarantee our future. I see myself as a small part of a much greater whole, and I completely subscribe to the notion that life is what you make it. There has been too much violence, too much ignorance, too much persecution in my family and among my ancestors. It fell on me to break the cycle if I wanted my life to be different.

Now, as I contemplate all the things I want to share, I am filled with indescribable joy. I love *me.* I accept me for who I am. A few semesters ago, a tall, dark and handsome student sat sideways in my classroom and carefully scrutinized every word I said. He asked very direct and provocative questions, and for a minute, I felt like J. Alfred Prufrock "sprawling on a pin." Those of us who teach know that there will always be a student who thinks he or she is smarter than the professor. I later learned, however, that he was a new father, a veteran, and he really wanted to know the answers to help guide him through all the newness. He sent me an email one day and asked me, "What is your definition of womanhood?" The summation of what I want to say to you lies in the answer I wrote back to him:

Bill:

According to my sources, the word 'womanhood' originated
in the 14th century as language transitioned from Old
to Middle English. It means 'qualities or characteristics
considered natural to a woman,' and its meaning of
'women collectively' started about 1520. Womanhood
is the feminine counterpart to manhood, which, in my
view, explains nothing. My sense, however, is that your
question is more philosophical and, therefore, commands

a philosophical answer. It is a question I have considered for many years, mostly because I have been called a 'WILD WOMAN', with the suggestion that I cannot be tamed. I embrace such a description of me, and because of that, I have had reasons to locate and identify that part of me that is peculiarly 'woman.' So, if your question can in any way be translated to 'What is a woman?' this is my take on it. I see this as an identification of myself.

A woman is the natural counterpart, gift, and complement to her man. She is a whole being—not fragmented into parts such as breasts, genitalia, hair and nails. She knows her role, and she knows herself. She makes sacrifices that even she does not recognize because she sees them as an innate part of her being. She gives freely, cries easily. When her man is strong, she surrenders. When he is weak, she supports him. If he is successful, she praises him. When he fails, she takes on his burdens and responsibilities. She loves hard with unbridled emotions. She is open—wide—even when she realizes that there is nothing worse than loving someone who constantly disappoints her. But when she closes…when she 'closes', the closing is permanent.

A woman is strong and strong-willed. She is conscious and determined. She is independent in the sense that she does not rely on her mate to provide her material needs. A woman is wife, mother, daughter, niece, teacher, economist, preacher, nurse, lover, friend, nurturer, and she is a fierce protectress. She is a bookkeeper, networker, organizer and cook. She is the vessel through which he perpetuates his manhood. Above all, she is an active participant in the development of her own mind, and this, I think, is the ESSENCE of woman.

This is also the reason why I am called 'wild.' I am conscious of the fact that I am intellectually superior to some. The 'traditional' role of being submissive and reliant, then, has never fit me. I know my own mind. I have been popped in the mouth and accused of 'competing' with my

man when, in truth, I was just being me. There is a line
in one of Tina Turner's songs which says, 'If you wanna
love a woman like me, it takes a MAN to do it' (emphasis
mine). I do recognize that my definition of woman is a
severe distinction from that of the 'little woman' or even
a little girl. Truly there is a child within all of us that we
never outgrow, and that is the good news to help us relate
to children. But a woman conquers and is strengthened by
adversity, and on the subject of life/survival, she does not
give in, she does not give out, and she does NOT give up.

All best,

Dr. B

Acknowledgments

I am truly grateful to Joe O'Connell, Professor of English at Austin Community College, for his encouragement and support. He read pages of the raw manuscript, offered suggestions, and assured me that the story is worth reading.

I want to thank my son, Jeremy Mitchell, and my grandson Aiden Doss, who either read portions of the book, or listened while I read it to them. Your input is priceless. Indeed, I am honored by the multitude of students who took interest in this project and always managed to find time in their busy schedules to discuss it with me. Namely, they are Yomara Hernandez, Jose Herrera Rocha, Laith Khireiwish, Maria Loaiza Zapata, and Alondra Nieves Munoz.

To my colleagues Dr. Carrza Dubose, Dr. Dania Dwyer and Dr. Latasha Goodwyn, I want to express my deepest gratitude for helping me survive the chaos.

Finally, Pam Booton, my advisor and sister/friend is always and in all ways my connection to sanity.

About Barbara Williams Lewis

BARBARA WILLIAMS LEWIS IS PROFESSOR OF ENGLISH at Austin Community College in Round Rock, Texas. She teaches Composition and American Literature. She earned her PhD in English at University of Southern California, where she focused on 20th Century African American Women Writers. Her first book, *Sherrod Village*, is a memoir that chronicles her journey to become educated.

When she is not writing, Dr. Lewis enjoys crocheting, making jewelry, and playing with her grandchildren. She lives near Austin, Texas.

Praise for *A WOMAN WILD*....

"*A Woman Wild* is a story that wins the readers' hearts. Great characters, images, and plot, evoking tears, laughter, curiosity, escape and inspiration. The book takes you into its world. You know when to smile, when to sigh, and when to duck!"

—Alamo Bay Press

www.ingramcontent.com/pod-product-compliance
Lightning Source LLC
Chambersburg PA
CBHW040223170726
48295CB00014B/784